Last Call

Last Call

A McLaughlin Romance

Shelli Stevens

Last Call

Tule Publishing First Printing, April 2018

The Tule Publishing Group, LLC

First Publication by Tule Publishing Group 2018

Second Edition

ISBN: 978-1-949068-14-6

Dedication

This story is dedicated to two friends I've lost in the past few years. To Trevon and to Colin. Colin worked at his family's pub—the Owl N' Thistle. Colin and his pub inspired characters in this series. Both of these men, whom I would easily call friends, will be sorely missed.

A huge thank you and virtual hug to my readers, and to Tule Publishing for giving this story a new home. And to the real Delonna whose name I stole and for all your info, and to all my friends at the Owl N' Thistle who gave me insight to the pub life!

Chapter One

WHERE THE *HELL* was her money?

Clothes flew into the air and out of her closet as Delonna cleared out every little inch of stuff, just in case.

In case what? In case she'd somehow misplaced the Folgers coffee container that was held shut by a large rubber band, stuffed in a pillowcase and surrounded by old T-shirts to hide it? Not fucking likely.

Panic and rage mixed now and she sank back onto the pile of clothes she'd just created. She stared into the closet, unblinking.

Tears of fury and frustration filled her eyes and she shook her head. Blonde hair spilled from her haphazard ponytail, falling in front of her face. She shoved it aside.

Her money was gone. Nearly six thousand dollars—in cash—that she'd saved over the years from her tips at the pub was gone. It had been there last night. She'd seen it when she'd gotten off shift and done her usual ritual of adding in her tips.

Which meant it had been taken today while she was

working. And there was no more denying it, it *had* been taken. It didn't matter how many times she checked the house, or searched her closet, the money wasn't going to suddenly reappear.

Fuck.

The possibility that this was a random robbery fleeted through her head, then right back out. It didn't make any sense. Nothing else in the house had been touched. Whoever had taken the money had known exactly what they were looking for.

And the only person who knew about her tips was Kenzie. Kenzie and… Oh, God. Realization sank in.

James.

Her boyfriend of over a year who hadn't visited, called, texted or really given any indication he was alive in over two weeks. Her boyfriend who had a key to the house.

Shock took her breath away and froze her tears. He wouldn't have done this to her, though. He couldn't have.

But if not him, then who?

A door slammed, followed by rushed footsteps.

"Delonna? Are you okay? I got your text."

Her friend and roommate appeared in the doorway a moment later. Kenzie just stared at her, before approaching slowly.

"Oh, honey, what's going on? Are you crying?"

Delonna couldn't even blink and her lower lip began to tremble. "Yeah. Actually, I'm pretty much on the verge of a full-scale breakdown."

"What happened? Is it that arse James?"

Most likely. Though her mind was having a hell of a time wrapping around that idea. What did sink in was that Kenzie had apparently never cared much for James if she'd just referred to him, in her very Scottish way, as an arse.

She managed a half nod, tried to explain and then gave a dry sob. Kenzie was at her side in an instant, kneeling in the pile of clothes and frowning with concern.

"Did the son of a bitch break your heart? Because you know I've three oversized brothers who probably wouldn't hesitate to break his face."

This time a watery laugh escaped as tears flowed freely down her cheeks now. She didn't doubt for a moment that Kenzie would sic the protective, intimidating McLaughlin men on James.

And Aleck, Kenzie's oldest brother, might be a little more inclined than any of them to take a personal interest in the situation. Only because Aleck was Delonna's boss, of course. Not because of one crazy day in summer where she'd lost her mind long enough to suck face with him.

Dumping that memory—that never seemed to vanish for long—she focused again on James and her stolen money.

He'd stolen her money. Not penny change, but a substantial amount. The thought circled around her head again, sinking in and growing more outlandish and shocking by the moment.

"My..." She drew in a ragged breath and glanced up at Kenzie. "My money is gone. I don't suppose you've seen it?"

"Your money?" Kenzie frowned and then her eyes went wide. "Oh shite! Not the tips you've been hoarding for years?"

Delonna nodded, not even cracking a smile at the use of the term hoarding. It had been their running joke since Kenzie had moved in almost a year ago. Kenzie was well aware of Delonna's super-tight budget and determination to save as much as possible. She'd always joked that Delonna was as stingy with her money as the Scottish.

"I've been at Brett's house," Kenzie murmured, guilt flushing her cheeks. "I've not been home in days. Maybe even a week. I suck, I know."

"You don't suck. You're in love," Delonna muttered absently.

No matter where she stayed, Kenzie always paid her rent. Though she'd finally admitted over the summer that she would be moving out in January to live with her fiancé. She'd been nice enough to give plenty of notice, unlike Delonna's last roommate who'd bailed immediately when she'd gotten a serious boyfriend.

They all left eventually, and usually for a guy.

"I need my phone." Delonna pushed herself to her feet, moving blindly through the house as she scrubbed the tears from her eyes.

She pulled it from her purse a moment later and opened

a blank message, loading James's name into the contact. Drawing in a deep breath, she hesitated and set her phone down on the table.

"You think it was James who took your money?" Kenzie had approached quietly from behind.

"You two were the only ones who knew about my tip stash. And I know you didn't take it."

"No," Kenzie agreed grimly. "I certainly didn't. Maybe you should call the police? I can text Colin."

"Don't get your brother involved. I don't want to involve the police. Yet." Delonna pursed her lips. "I only reported half of my tips to the IRS and if I report that kind of money missing… I just don't want to get into any trouble. And I don't have any proof James took it."

"Are you going try and get it back?"

"I'm going to sure as hell try."

"How?" Kenzie pulled out a chair at the kitchen table and urged her to sit down. "Is he dangerous? I don't know James very well. I'll admit it. Every time he's around he keeps to himself quite a bit."

"I don't think he'd ever hurt me, if that's what you mean. And he's not much of an extrovert." An understatement.

Delonna sank down into the chair. The standoffish, angry, dangerous vibe about him was what had drawn her to him in the first place. The sex had been really good, but their relationship—though lasting over a year—had functioned on a shallow level.

And yet you gave him a key to your house.

"Are you going to call him?"

"He's not going to answer my calls or texts if he's guilty of taking my money."

"So you're going to see him? Show up at his door?"

"I don't think I can. Not today at least. I have to be at work in two hours, and I couldn't get to Seattle and back by then."

Getting to Seattle meant either driving the length of the island, taking the ferry and then some more driving, or heading over the Deception Pass Bridge and driving for almost two hours. Either way, she didn't have time.

Or enough gas money now. What she had was the $180 in tips from last night and a pretty depressing checking account that she used mainly to pay bills.

"Call in sick."

Delonna snorted. "Your brother would kill me for leaving him hanging. It's Saturday night."

"You wouldn't leave him hanging. There're at least two other bartenders who'd love to take your shift and make some weekend money."

"You think?"

"I know. Call CJ. He'll cover, I'm sure of it. He was just telling me how he wanted to pick up some extra shifts."

"You're working tonight, right?"

Kenzie nodded. "Aye."

"Will you back up my bullshit story about being sick?"

With her expression grim, Kenzie gave another nod. "Definitely. That teriyaki chicken you ate at lunch gave you an absolute nightmare case of the runs."

Delonna let out a crack of laughter. "Do *not* tell your brother I had the runs, or so help me God—"

"Vomiting is preferable?"

"Slightly. Oh damn, whatever. Just, whatever you go with, make it convincing."

"Oh, aye. I'm fantastic at this kind of thing." Kenzie paused. "I wish you'd bring someone with you, though. A man, preferably. Just to be safe."

James wouldn't hurt her. He wouldn't be that fucking stupid.

"I'll be fine," she said resolutely. "Besides, if something *does* happen to me, you'll point the police in his direction."

Kenzie's eyes widened. "Is that supposed to make me feel better?"

"No. Just being a realist."

Folding her arms over her chest, Kenzie huffed. "Well I don't much care for your realism."

"I'm sure. How about I text you and check in throughout the night so you know I'm okay?"

"You'd bloody well better… Maybe I could have Brett go with you—"

"No." Delonna stood. "I'm going alone."

Kenzie sighed. "All right. Don't do anything stupid."

"Would I do that?"

"Actually, knowing you, aye. You just might. You think with your emotions, sometimes, not your brain. And you're young and impulsive."

"I'm twenty-four, and now you're just being mean." Delonna grimaced, grabbing her purse.

"Don't get pissy, you know I'm right."

"I do," she agreed softly and hugged Kenzie. "Thanks for covering for me. I'll call CJ on the way."

Driving off the island a half hour later, she couldn't help but think about how right Kenzie was. The reason she was in this situation right now was because she hadn't been using her head, but her heart. Okay, maybe not heart. Vagina was more accurate.

Shaking her head, she knew she might just try to kick James square in the junk when she saw him. They were close in height—so what if he had fifty pounds of muscle on her?

If he really had taken her money, she was going to make sure as shit he regretted it.

ALECK GLANCED AROUND the pub, which was only moderately busy this time of night. Fewer than half the tables were occupied and a few regulars lingered at the bar counter, sipping their beers and watching the game on the flat-screens.

It was the calm before the storm. He knew this town,

and his pub, well enough to realize it would be standing room only in a few hours.

By then he'd be out of here. Off at nine and out to dinner with a pretty lady. What was her name again? Melissa? Michelle? Shite, did it really matter? By the end of the night they'd likely be shagging their brains out.

She was a regular at the pub and had been coming on strong for months now—making it plain and clear she wouldn't mind bringing him back to her place.

Though she was pretty enough, he wouldn't have been interested had she not made the first move. But seeing that it had been several months since he'd been with a woman, it was probably damn well time to break the dry spell.

"Evening, boss."

He glanced over to see CJ striding up to the counter, a shit-eating grin on his face.

"CJ." Aleck nodded and arched a brow. "Tell me you haven't come to spend your free evening at your place of employment?"

"I'm working." CJ stepped behind the counter. "Delonna asked me to cover her shift."

Aleck blinked as he digested that shocking statement. "Delonna did?"

"Yup. She didn't call you?"

His jaw flexed. "No. I've not heard a word from her."

Delonna never called in sick. Never failed to show up for a shift.

"Did she happen to say why?"

CJ shrugged, not appearing altogether concerned. "Said she was sick or some shit. Doesn't matter to me. I just heard dollar signs."

The bigger crowds on the weekends tended to bring in bigger tips. Friday and Saturday night shifts were always sought after by his employees. For Delonna to have given up a shift must've meant she was truly sick.

Concern flitted through him and he bit back a curse. For the first time in months he was going to have a bit of fun, and yet now that thought was replaced with the vision of Delonna violently ill.

Across the room, he spotted Kenzie making her way into the pub for her shift, which began in a half hour. Setting down the bar rag, he strode toward her.

"Kenzie. A word?"

His sister glanced toward him and gave a brief smile. "Sure."

She kept walking to the back, not appearing worried or curious about why he was asking to talk. Then again there really was no reason he'd pick a fight with her—not anymore. Over the summer they'd butted heads more than once over the man she'd begun dating. The man who was now her fiancé.

Brett Craven was a good man, and now that Aleck had gotten to know him he could admit the two were not only well matched, but also deeply in love.

Closing the door to the back office, he turned to face her.

"And how are you this evening, big brother?" She grabbed a pen off his desk and began tapping it against her palm.

"Just lovely. It's Delonna I'm concerned about."

"Oh, you've heard she's sick then?"

"Aye. What's wrong with her?"

Kenzie didn't miss a beat. "I've just told you. She's sick."

"You've seen her? How is she?"

"We had teriyaki chicken for lunch. Some dodgy place that just opened near the Navy base. Unfortunately it hasn't sat well with her."

"She's got food poisoning then?"

"Aye. Quite terribly really. She's still being sick, last I heard."

"Sounds bloody awful. How did you avoid getting poisoning too if you ate at the same place?"

Kenzie's gaze slid away. "She had the chicken, whereas fortunately I chose the shrimp skewers. Sadly, she couldn't have known that decision would change her plans from working a busy shift to hugging a porcelain god."

Aleck's scowl deepened. "And you left her alone?"

"*I* have to work, Aleck." Kenzie gave an amused laugh. "It won't do to have us both short of rent next month."

"Delonna's short on rent?"

She stared at him for a minute, and he could see her mentally backtracking. The wheels in her head spinning.

"She's fine. I was just making a joke, since she's missing work tonight."

Maybe. But he knew his sister well enough to know she'd just admitted more than she wanted. Was Delonna struggling financially? That seemed impossible. The woman brought in more tips than any other bartender or waitress who worked here. She was funny, sexy and personable. The customers adored her. She shouldn't have been hurting for money. Was she blowing it somewhere?

The pressing urge to check on her only grew. Perhaps he could swing by before his date with Melissa. Or was it Michelle? Hell. He would really have to figure out her name before he saw her tonight.

"Ah, well the poor lass. Maybe I'll pop by and bring her a couple cans of ginger ale and some soda bread."

There was silence and when he glanced up Kenzie just blinked at him.

"Don't do that."

Baffled, he shook his head. "And why the fook not?"

"Why would you do that? She's just your employee. It would be weird," Kenzie said tersely. "Would you bring CJ ginger ale and soda bread?"

"Aye. Maybe." Not a chance in hell, actually.

"She's in no condition to be seen, Aleck. Probably looks like arse, smells like rotten eggs—"

"You don't eat shrimp." He stared at her, that realization hitting quite suddenly. "You hate all shellfish. Always have."

That same look of backtracking flashed across his sister's face. "Time for a hearing aid already? I didn't say shrimp, I said beef."

"The fook you did." He scrutinized her and reached his conclusion. "You're lying. Covering for her. Where is Delonna really?"

Kenzie folded her arms across her chest and tossed her red hair. "I've told you already. She's sick."

"All right." He nodded. "Fine. Well I'll still be dropping by to wish her well then."

He turned and moved to the door. Clearly she was trying to call his bluff, because only when his hand touched the handle did she call out, "Wait!"

Chapter Two

ALECK TURNED AND arched a brow at his sister. "The truth."

"People lie and call in sick all the time, Aleck," she said curtly. "I hardly think you'd go through this much trouble to find the real reason with anyone else. It's not as if she's done this before."

It didn't matter if her points were valid. "The truth, Kenzie. Is she with her boyfriend?"

Her eyes narrowed and she set the pen back on his desk. "And would it matter if she was?"

"If she skipped work—"

"It doesn't matter, she made sure her shift was covered. You're hardly in a bind here."

"It's the principle."

"Really? And you hold all your employees to that level of principle?" Kenzie heaved a sigh. "If so, then you should probably know I called in sick two weeks ago, so that Brett and I could keep shagging without me having to leave halfway through the evening."

"Kenzie!"

"What?" Her eyes widened innocently. "You started this."

Dammit all, but he didn't want to even *think* about his sister having a sex life.

She approached him, her gaze searching his. "What's this really about, Aleck? Why are you taking such a personal interest in Delonna?"

His teeth snapped together and he met her stare grimly. Just how much did his nosy little sister know? Had Delonna told her about that brief lapse in sanity between the two of them over the summer?

That night was still clear in his head. He'd dropped by to check on her well-being after she'd been injured, and she'd answered the door clearly expecting someone else. Likely her boyfriend—because she'd answered the door in tiny panties and a tank top. His concern had turned to desire, and before he knew it he'd been exploring the inside of her mouth with his tongue.

Would Delonna have confided that moment—one they agreed would go on record as never having happened—to his sister?

No. Staring down at Kenzie, he knew Delonna would be just as determined as he was to keep that moment quiet.

"She's been employed at my pub for several years now," he finally answered briskly. "She's also your roommate. So, aye, she falls under my umbrella of protection."

"*Those* are your reasons for being protective?" Kenzie finally shook her head. "Okay. Sure. You go ahead and tell yourself that, and I'll pretend to buy it."

"What the fook does that mea—?"

"Here's the deal. She went to confront James tonight after he may or may not have stolen a shite-ton of money from her tips that she's been saving up."

The blood in his body went from simmering with irritation to an icy chill. He pulled up the image of Delonna's boyfriend in his mind. Average height, bulky and muscled, with a beard and tattoos. He rode a motorcycle, if he remembered correctly. Aleck rarely generalized, and had plenty of biker friends, but it wouldn't surprise him to learn James was involved in one of those dodgy biker gangs.

"How much money?" It had to be quite a bit if Delonna had gone to confront him. "Hundreds?"

Kenzie hesitated. "I don't know how much, exactly. But I'm thinking thousands. Over five."

"She had thousands of dollars in cash just lying around? What the bloody hell was she thinkin'?" he roared, pressing a hand to his forehead.

"It wasn't lying around, you arse, it was well hidden. And I'm not telling you this so you can judge her, I'm telling you this because I'm worried."

He had been too, but to hear his sister voice the same fear… *Shite.* "You think he'd hurt her?"

"I really don't know. I just don't trust him. I never have.

But she was...happy enough. So it wasn't my business." She sighed. "I tried to convince her to take a guy with her tonight, and would've been happy to ask Brett if she'd let me."

"I'll go after her."

"You have no idea where he lives."

Aleck pushed past her, muttering, "As if that would stop me."

DELONNA WAS ON the ferry, in the middle of Puget Sound, when Aleck's text came in.

Where are you?

She exited the game she'd been playing on her phone, and stared down at the message. Quickly, she typed a response.

In bed, sick to my stomach, boss boy. Didn't CJ tell you?

Shit. Was he going to get all pissy because she'd called in sick? It was maybe the second time she'd ever done so in her time working at the pub.

Her phone buzzed again.

Cut the bullshit. I know about the missing money and you heading to Seattle. Where are you?

What the *hell*? Kenzie had ratted her out? Disappointment and anger flashed through her, and she tossed her phone onto the passenger seat.

How did she even answer that? Better yet, why should she have to? She wasn't Aleck's responsibility.

Dammit.

She picked up her phone again and texted Kenzie.

You told him?

The text came back a moment later, as if Kenzie had been waiting to hear from her.

I'm so sorry, he completely called my bluff and bullied it out of me. You know how he can be. And he's worried about you—we both are.

Delonna tossed her phone back onto the passenger seat. Well, let them worry. She didn't have time to coddle and reassure them she'd be okay. Yes, James had likely stolen a shit-ton of money from her and she was beyond enraged, but she really didn't think he'd hurt her during the confrontation.

They'd dated for over a year, slept together every chance they'd gotten—and she was banking on a shaky relationship combined with good sex being grounds to talk about this reasonably.

The ferry began to dock, and her attention shifted from James to her plan of action once she got to his house. A plan of action that included...what now? Use her key—like hell she'd give him a chance to not answer her knock—enter his apartment and then kick him square in the nuts. Then begin questioning.

Yeah, that sounded pretty good.

Five minutes later she was off the ferry and heading toward I5. Well on her way to James's place. Her phone hadn't stopped buzzing, but she didn't check to see if the messages were from Kenzie or Aleck. Right now she couldn't be bothered with either of them.

When she arrived at James's complex, she didn't automatically spot his truck, but no matter. She'd wait for his sorry ass to get home if need be. But just in case he was avoiding her, she'd park around the corner to avoid tipping off her presence here.

She'd gotten a late start heading to Seattle—grabbing a quick shower and food first—and it was already close to eight. So really, he should've been off work from his customer service job.

He's probably out blowing your money. Right this very moment.

Her stomach roiled as she slid out of the car. She wrapped her arms around her chest, shivering in the October evening air. This knock-off North Face fleece wasn't doing shit to keep her warm. But she was too cheap to buy the real deal.

She reached the complex quickly and climbed the outdoor stairs to the second floor. Her footsteps echoed, and she couldn't help but notice how deserted it seemed. There was literally no one around. Several apartments had lights on, but it was just graveyard quiet.

Gripping her keys in her hand, she stopped outside his apartment. Even through the blinds she could tell it was dark inside. So it was looking more likely that he wasn't home. Fine. She'd kill some time watching TV. James had all the cable channels, which was a luxury she'd never indulged in.

She unlocked the door and pushed it open, hitting the light switch as she walked inside. Despite knowing he wasn't home, she still called out his name tentatively. There was no reply, of course.

She closed the door and walked down the hall to the living room, thinking it wasn't much warmer inside than outside.

When she reached the end of the hall she gave a strangled gasp. It was empty. No big leather couch. No giant television. No side table. The room was absolutely empty except for a candy bar wrapper in the middle of a carpet that was direly in need of a good vacuuming.

No. This wasn't happening.

Forcing herself to keep moving, she rushed down the hall to the one bedroom in the apartment. The door was open, and a quick glance inside showed it just as empty.

Her stomach sank and the thick, cloying sense of dread swelled heavier inside her. With trembling fingers, she pulled her cell phone free from her purse. Ignoring the list of texts on the lock screen, she went to her contacts, found James and hit dial. It went straight to voicemail.

"Shit." She leaned against the wall, not trusting her legs to hold her up for much longer.

He was gone. He was fucking *gone*. And his phone was off.

She sank to the carpeted ground and closed her eyes against the tears of shock. Why? Why had he done this to her?

She was so lost in her own miserable world that it took her a moment to recognize the sound of the door to the apartment opening.

Hadn't she shut it? Locked it? No. Realization kicked in. She hadn't locked the door.

Her insides twisted as the despair slid into fear. What were the chances it was James returning to the abandoned apartment? Not very likely.

Footsteps sounded in the apartment now. Unhurried and light—almost as if the person were trying to be quiet. With nothing but silence surrounding her, though, he may as well have been stomping.

She glanced around, frantically searching for anything she could use as a weapon. Nothing. There was literally nothing but a candy bar wrapper. James had a horrible sugar habit.

Spotting the open closet just feet from her, she moved to her hands and knees and crawled as quickly as she could over and into it. As much as she wanted to close the door, she knew the sound would tip off whoever was in here.

The footsteps stopped and she caught her breath, hope flaring inside her.

Turn and leave. There's nobody here.

Almost a minute of silence, before the footsteps sounded again. This time they were coming down the hall.

Fuck. Shit. Damn. Delonna let out every curse she knew in her head as she glanced around the closet, hoping to find a weapon of sorts. Nothing but a plastic hanger. It'd have to do.

She grabbed it and slowly rose to her feet. Maybe whomever it was would just glance in the room and not bother to check the closet. If they just peeked in the room, they wouldn't be able to see her…

The footsteps moved into the room. Closer. Closer still. She'd be in view in just about any—

Delonna slammed the hanger down onto the hand that reached into the closet.

"*Ouch.*"

Ignoring the furious, blatantly male cry of pain, she darted past him and sprinted straight for the front door to the apartment. An iron-like arm slammed around her waist, stopping her momentum and snapping her backward into a solid chest.

"Oof." The air rushed from her and her head spun from the impact of hitting wide, hard shoulders. The shock subsided and panic kicked in again.

She tried to elbow him, head-butt him, kick him, do something to free herself. Nothing worked, because he held her too tight and dodged her blows.

"Delonna, stop it." The snarled words finally registered. "Stop fookin' struggling. It's me. Aleck."

Aleck. The tension fled her body as relief sank in. She went limp in his grip and her heart slowed back to normal. Her breath was shuddering, before she tried to pull out of his grip again. This time he let her go.

Stunned disbelief had her turning and demanding, "What in the hell are you doing here?"

His gaze flickered with irritation. "Keepin' your arse out of trouble."

She was already so on the edge, that his close proximity made her even more off-balance. His nearly black hair, vivid green eyes and perfect smile could take a girl's breath away, while his broad-shouldered, nearly six-and-a-half-foot frame was enough to intimidate.

She stepped back from him, trying to get her heart rate back under control. "How did you even find me? Find James's apartment?"

Not that he lived here anymore. Clearly.

"I got his full name from Kenzie, and had Colin look him up in the system."

Of course Kenzie had given that information freely. And so why wouldn't Aleck have his brother, a sheriff's detective on the island, look up James?

Her mouth flattened. "That's a hell of a lot of trouble you went through to figure out where my boyfriend lives."

"So he's still your boyfriend, aye?" Aleck's gaze slid around the apartment. "After he's stolen your money and skipped town. You certainly know how to choose them."

"Well that kind of reply is going to garner you a big old *fuck you*, Aleck. Go ahead and judge me from your high horse. Or wait a minute, don't. In fact I'd appreciate it if you'd stay the hell out of my personal business."

With a glare meant to wither his balls, she turned and strode out of the bedroom.

AH, FOOK IT all.

Aleck strode after her, his brisk strides bringing him to the front door before she arrived at it. He blocked her exit and softened his expression.

"I apologize. That was a shite thing to say," he said tightly.

She met his gaze. The anger in her eyes hadn't settled even a little bit. "Yes, it was."

"I was worried about you. We all were." He shook his head. "It doesn't seem wise for you to confront a man who was obviously desperate enough to steal a large sum of money from you. Even if he was your boyfriend." He narrowed his eyes. "Unless you're giving him the benefit of the doubt and calling him your lover still."

She gave a laugh that was half exasperation and half despondency. "No. He's definitely no longer welcome in my bed, and clearly it's hard to give him the benefit of the doubt when only he and Kenzie knew about the money. And then—" she gestured around the abandoned apartment "—this."

Staring down at her, he watched the panic and disbelief fill her eyes again. Saw her body begin to tremble and tears gather. She looked vulnerable, and so damn young. Which, really, she still was.

Something inside him softened and the urge to pull her into an embrace hit hard. Which didn't settle well with him—not after that sensual moment at her place two months ago. Touching her in any way or form was best to be avoided.

Instead of reaching for her, he offered a gruff, "Let's get you out of here, Lana."

The area between her brows wrinkled. "What did you call me?"

Shite, had he called her the name aloud? Lana had been the nickname in his head for a while now, but he'd never let it slip. Then again, during the past few months their working relationship had shifted. Had become not quite so employer and employee. Though he wasn't sure how he'd qualify what it had become.

Sliding a gaze over her, he took in her blonde hair that was nearly out of the low ponytail, the thick, cream, knit sweater that fell to her thighs, and then the tight jeans that were tucked into calf-high brown boots.

It suited her girl-next-door persona and sexy-without-trying appearance right now.

"Just a nickname," he murmured. "Didn't realize I'd even used it."

She gave a shrug, her mind clearly elsewhere again. "It's fine, it just surprised me more than anything. My family used to call me that. I was named after my mom's best friend."

Her words grew fainter as she glanced around the apartment. The shock and helplessness in her eyes made him realize she was still trying to digest what she was seeing.

"You'll not be able to sort out anything here," he said quietly. "Let's go find some place to grab a coffee. Sweets. Something."

He just needed to get her out of here. With the appearance of this apartment being abandoned, two people wandering around inside would only draw unwanted attention.

Delonna finally nodded. "You're right. I need to sit down and get my head on straight. I can't do that here."

She turned and moved away from him, making a beeline for the door, leaving Aleck rushing to keep up with her.

"I'm sorry if I freaked you guys out," she muttered, giving him a quick glance. "I'll just head home. You really don't need to waste any more of your Saturday night on me."

"I've no plans." *Blatant lie.* He stayed by her side. "And you're not exactly in any state to be driving. Coffee first. I insist."

"You insist?" She arched a brow and waited as he stepped out onto the walkway outside of the apartment, then shut the door and locked it with a key. "And what if I still said no?"

"Then I'll throw you over my shoulder, toss you into my car and personally drive you to coffee." He paused. "Kidding, of course."

"Of course." Her lips quirked as they walked down the stairs and to the parking lot together.

He glanced around the parking lot. "Where's your car? I didn't see it driving in."

"I parked on a side road. I didn't want to alert James to my presence. I'll just grab it and meet you...where did you say you wanted to go?"

"I didn't." He frowned, not liking the idea of her driving off alone right now. "Why don't you ride with me and I'll bring you back in a bit?"

Her steps faltered and she shook her head, but didn't say no. The utterly lost look in her eyes had his heart clenching.

"Don't overthink it, Lana." He caught her hand and tugged her toward his car. She didn't resist and a moment later was seated in the passenger seat.

He climbed behind the wheel, started the vehicle and drove them out of the parking lot. While he'd promised her coffee in Seattle, he wasn't sure where the fook to go. He was an island boy now, and rarely left Whidbey except on random outings. And now he was supposed to take her to a coffee house? Shite, he'd probably just end up at a Starbucks.

Fortunately, several miles down the road, his lights cut through the drizzle and landed on a coffee shop in a small plaza. And they were still open—which was quite the difference from Whidbey where so many places closed by nine.

Delonna had remained silent on the short drive, and when he cast a glance her way, her eyes were closed. Despite the tension around her mouth and brows drawn together, she managed to look utterly exhausted.

"We're here." He probably needn't have announced it, but she didn't seem to be in any hurry to move. "And I think you may need a triple shot."

She opened her eyes, turned her head against the seat and gave a hint of a smile. "Of vodka? You're on."

"Espresso, you cheeky drunk," he teased lightly.

"Well nobody ever said you were a good time, boss boy."

"I'm an incredibly good time, not that you'd know."

"Mmm hmm."

Their teasing, easygoing dynamics were natural and fell easily into place. Under the hint of streetlight, their gazes didn't move from each other. Something shifted and something flickered in her eyes. A memory. An awareness.

She lowered her lashes and glanced away, unbuckling her

seat belt. A moment later she had her door open and slid out, muttering, "Let's get that coffee."

He followed her out of his car and set the locks behind him. With her walking in front of him, it gave him an unwanted moment to briefly slide his gaze over the brilliant curve of her arse.

And you're a bastart for noticing.

"Ooo La Latte?" She glanced back at him. "Hmm. Let's see if the coffee is as good as the name."

The interior of the coffee shop was cozy with gentle lighting. There were soft leather chairs and a couch, and then smaller tables spread about. Paper star lanterns hung over the tables, casting a fun and intimate light.

The tempting smell of coffee beans hit his nostrils and he drew in a deep breath, appreciating it. Generally he was a tea drinker, but now and then he enjoyed a good coffee beverage—so long as it was blended with enough sugary things.

"What'll you have? I'll order it for you, if you'll grab us a table?"

She glanced at the chalkboard menu on the wall. "Get me a large pumpkin latte—with those two extra shots. And thanks."

While she wandered off to grab a corner table, he ordered their drinks—choosing the same drink she had, minus the extra shots. He was already wired enough.

As the barista made their drinks, a thought slid through his head. Right about now he should've been on the island, shagging his date. It was the first time he'd really dwelled on it since making the decision to go after Delonna.

Did he regret it?

He thought about it for a moment, considered what could be happening and what was happening instead. He slid a glance over to Delonna. Her elbows were on the table and she had her palms pressed against her forehead. She'd taken her hair all the way out of the ponytail and it fell over her shoulder now.

She looked vulnerable, and somehow angry as fook. Despite his determination to never go there in his head again, he thought back on that moment a couple months ago.

He'd been lightly cupping her face, stroking a finger down her jaw and trying like mad to maintain control and not act on the alarming instinct to kiss her. And then she'd taken the choice out of his hands by pressing her soft, lush body against him and kissing him first.

Then he'd lost control. *Then* he'd kissed the ever-lovin' hell out of her. And at least once a day since then, he wondered what it would've been like if they hadn't stopped.

As he stared at her, Delonna's gaze lifted and ran from his toes to the top of his head. When she finally met his stare, a hint of a guilty smile curved her lips before she looked away.

He made a soft grunt as their order was called, and hid a smile of his own. No. There were definitely no regrets about coming after her tonight.

Chapter Three

GREAT. AS IF Aleck's ego wasn't big enough, he'd just caught her checking him out.

And, sadly, after a few moments she couldn't stop herself from sneaking another glance at him. Fortunately he was collecting their drinks.

Though no one would blame her for looking at Aleck McLaughlin. There was no doubt about it—the man was sex on a stick. And more and more lately she'd been tempted to take a lick. Which had been pretty shitty of her, seeing as she had a boyfriend.

Had being the keyword now. *Mother fucking son of a bitch.* God, she wanted to cut off his balls and shove them down his throat. She couldn't think about it. The more she thought about how screwed she was, the more depressed and despondent she got.

"Your pumpkin latte."

She glanced at the steaming cup of fragrant coffee, and then up at him.

"Thank you." After wrapping her hands around the hot

porcelain, she lifted it to her lips and took a small sip.

"Is it as good as the name of the shop?"

She glanced up through her lashes and found his gaze on her. Or more so, her mouth. The dark heat in his eyes warmed her belly more than the coffee. Feeling strangely unsettled, she gave a nervous laugh.

"It's even better. Best pumpkin latte I've had, hands down."

"I'll agree. Though to be honest, this is my first."

"A virgin, hmm?" And why had she said that? Flirting was second nature to her, but she had to watch herself with Aleck nowadays.

Sure enough, when she made the mistake of catching his gaze, his eyes were alight with amusement and a hint of lazy awareness.

"Aye, and maybe the only area in my life I can actually say that."

Her heart did a little flip and she swallowed against the butterflies in her stomach. More and more lately he'd been making her feel like this—the kiss had only made it worse.

And it was wrong on so many levels, because fantasizing about your boss could only be trouble. And clearly she had enough trouble as it was.

"Why not use a bank?"

She blinked, struggling to focus on and understand his question.

"A bank."

"For your money."

She snapped right back to reality. He must've realized the dangerous waters of their conversation and changed the topic. Mission accomplished. The last thing on her mind now was getting it on with Aleck.

"I use a bank." She gave a small shrug. "But I prefer to use cash for spending money. To have some around in case of an emergency, or, you know, if something catastrophic happened."

"I'm not sure cash will be in demand during the zombie apocalypse, but you're probably smart to have it anyway."

An honest laugh escaped her and she allowed a small smile. "Well, I was thinking more devastating earthquake, but zombie apocalypse works too."

"You're quite morbid, you realize that."

"I'm practical. I'll bet you don't even have an emergency food and water stash."

"I've more liquor than I know what to do with."

"At the pub, I'm sure, but do you plan to live there and indulge in vodka martinis?"

"And why not? Sounds like a champion way to go out as you're warding off zombies." His grin slipped a little. "That's a very mature way of thinking, by the way. Having so much money saved on hand. Having so much money saved at all really."

Her mouth tightened. "I'm not ten."

"No, that you're not." He gave a somewhat forced laugh.

"What I'm saying is that most women in their early twenties seem to be more concerned about having fun, or are off at college."

"I don't have the desire or money to go to college right now." Her slight smile slid down into a frown. "I make a lot of money working as a bartender. While those in college are accruing debt, I'm accruing savings. Or was, anyway. And, besides, you know I enjoy my job."

He gave a small nod, and there was no judgment in his gaze. "Aye. You do."

She didn't add what else she'd been saving the money for. Who knew how he'd react? Maybe he'd be irritated. Discouraging. Either way, she didn't want to deal with it.

Sliding her gaze back to her drink, she took another sip.

"I assume you'll file a report with the police?"

Her hand clenched around the cup at Aleck's quiet question.

"I don't know. I hate to involve them." She met his gaze warily. "I didn't report all my tips to the IRS."

"I'm fairly sure that's quite common for people in our industry. It shouldn't stop you from going to the police. I hardly think Colin will turn you in to the IRS." His lips twitched, before he grew serious again. "You need to file a report, Lana."

Her stomach clenched. Kenzie had said the same thing. "I know. I will."

"Good. I'll text Colin and give him a heads-up that

you'll be coming by the station."

Her head whipped up and she met his knowing gaze. He'd essentially called her bluff, and she *had* been bluffing.

"This wasn't penny change taken from you. You can't allow the bastart to get away with this."

Bastart. God, when his Scottish accent thickened and he dropped little words that were so clearly not local, she got a bit shivery.

Focus on the meaning of the words, Delonna, not how he says them. He was right. As much as she didn't want to involve the police, she'd be stupid not to.

"I know." She nodded. "Go ahead and text Colin. That'd be great, actually."

Aleck nodded and slipped his phone out of his pocket, deftly typing and sending a text. He looked up a moment later. "I'll follow you home tonight."

"Follow me home?" Her brows rose. "Why?"

"Just to make sure you're safe. Kenzie is working late, though I'm not quite sure she'd even be there anyway from what I understand."

"No, she goes to Brett's more often than not now." She finished her drink, a little sad that the last delicious drop was gone. "But I'll be fine. Really, there's no need—"

"This isn't up for debate."

She gave a faint smile. "You're kind of a bully."

"Aye, it wouldn't be the first time I was told that." He finished his drink and set the cup down. "Shall we?"

"Yeah. I guess we'd better."

They stood and walked out together, waving goodbye to the friendly barista, who wished them a good night.

When they arrived back outside James's apartment, her stomach had that leaden feeling again and another wave of misery swept through her. All that money. Gone. Along with the man she'd dated for over a year. Clearly her instincts in judging people were for shit.

"You sure you're okay to drive?"

She gave a humorless smile and glanced over at Aleck. "I'm not full of alcohol, just self-loathing."

His brows furrowed and he opened his mouth to say something, but she didn't want to hear it.

She climbed out of the car and called out, "See you in my rearview, boss boy."

ALECK HELD HER to that promise. He ensured they were never separated by more than one or two cars, keeping her taillights in his vision at all times.

They were lucky in their timing and drove onto one of the ferries with only a few minutes' wait. She didn't go upstairs during the crossing, but sat in her car, so he did the same.

He tapped his fingers on the steering wheel and stared at her through her back window. She looked as if she were asleep with her head back against the headrest and not moving.

Full of self-loathing, she'd said. Why? She was too hard on herself. Aleck hadn't much cared for her boyfriend, but he couldn't have predicted the arse would do this kind of thing. Some people were just shoddy pricks.

The boat pulled into the dock and she shifted in her seat, clearly awake now.

As they drove off the boat and onto the island, the first thick raindrops hit his windshield. Shite. Nothing like driving in a heavy rainstorm at night, on the dark tree-lined roads of the island. He slowed down, knowing deer could dart across the road at any point. Delonna seemed to be in a similar mindset and decreased her speed as well.

By the time they reached the busier and artificially brighter side of the island—Oak Harbor—it was nearing midnight. Aleck pulled his car into the driveway behind her and climbed out. Delonna was already halfway to the door and cast him a backward glance.

"I made it. Thanks for the escort, but you can head out now."

"Aye, you made it to your front porch, but I'll see you safely inside if you don't mind."

Under the porch light he saw a flash of uncertainty in her eyes, but then her lashes fell and she nodded. "Always the gentleman."

"I try."

She unlocked her door and stepped inside. He followed

just steps behind her.

When she hit the lights, they both looked around the interior. Not sure what he'd expected to find, he was relieved to see everything in close range appeared to be in order. Without a word, he stepped past her and moved through the house, checking each room and closet for a sign of anyone.

"No one's here," she called out, exasperation in her words. "Well, besides us."

Without acknowledging her protest, he opened the door to another room and slid his gaze over it.

"Wait, don't go in there."

Aleck stumbled to the side as she shoved and then dove past him into the room. He watched in dismay as she knocked some kind of long, cylindrical pink thing off the nightstand.

Shaking his head, he muttered, "What the—"

"Nothing. You saw nothing."

"Actually, I'm quite sure I just saw your vibrator."

"You saw nothing, dammit!"

He couldn't help but laugh as her face turned scarlet.

"There's no shame in masturbation, Lana. I'll not be judging you or your Naughty Rabbit, Pink Wand of Pleasure, Tantric Teaser, or whatever it is you call it—"

"Shut the fuck up!" Eyes wide with mortification, Delonna glared at him. "And I take back everything I just said about you being a gentleman."

His lips quirked as he made an effort to contain his

smile. So Delonna was into toys, aye? Did that mean she embraced her kinky side?

He suddenly recalled her making some joke, months back, about Aleck turning her over his knee and her liking it. He'd nearly gone hard at the time thinking about that scenario. But maybe she'd just been teasing to get him riled. And maybe the vibrator was just relief because her boyfriend wasn't getting the job done.

The image of her getting it on with James made him a bit irritable, so he pushed that thought from his mind. But the idea of her spending some alone time with the toy…

"Nice. And now you've got that look in your eyes," she accused, shoving past him and out of the room again.

Shite. He didn't bother to ask what look, because he knew what look. The look that clearly spelled out just what he'd been envisioning.

"As you can see, the house is empty. So while I appreciate all you've done, it's probably time for you to go."

"Probably," he agreed and backed out of her room, closing the door behind him.

He followed her to the front door, where she held it open and waited for him to leave.

Pausing at the door, he glanced down at her. "You'll be all right then?"

Her humiliation seemed to subside as she sighed and gave a small nod. "I'll be fine. Thank you for being concerned about me tonight enough to follow me to Seattle and back."

All right, it sounded a little extreme when she put it that way.

"I was concerned. Still am."

"I'll be fine."

Her blue-green-hazel eyes clouded and there was a flicker of unease in them.

"You will be fine," he agreed and reached out to draw the backs of two fingers down her cheek.

The gesture was meant to be reassuring, but the air between them came instantly alive with something else.

For a moment he was thrown back to that day over the summer when they'd been in a similar position. When she'd stared at him with heat in her eyes, before she'd gone up on her tiptoes and kissed him.

Every muscle in his body went taut at the memory of how her lips had felt beneath his. The seductive spontaneity and sensuality of it all. Later, she'd blamed it on the prescription pain meds she'd been given.

It was a plausible explanation. Maybe. Or maybe she'd just wanted to kiss him. Delonna had always been a harmless flirt with everyone. But mostly with him.

He heard the shift in her breathing, as if she felt the sudden change in the air between them too. Felt the thick, swirling sexual tension. The pull of another impending kiss.

Instinct had him lowering his head and her lashes swept down again. The hand on his chest made him pause.

"You need to go." Her words were husky. Uneven. For a moment, disorientation claimed him. Then he remembered where they were and all that had happened tonight. Shite.

"Aye. I'll be on my way." He stepped back from her and gave a small nod. "Call if you need anything."

"I will," she promised. "Night, boss boy."

"Good night, Lana."

Without a backward glance, he turned and left the house. The door closed, and the slide of the dead bolt sounded.

Good girl.

Chapter Four

SUNDAY EVENING IN the bar was dead. The crowd who'd come in to watch the Seahawks game had gone home for the evening, and the pub held only a handful of regulars now.

"It'll pick up."

Delonna glanced over at Aleck as he made his way down the bar toward her. She hoped it would, and usually it did somewhat during the dinner rush.

"I hope so." She sighed. "I have a lot of money I need to replenish."

His gaze narrowed, the expression in his eyes one of concern. "Did you file a report with the sheriff?"

She arched a brow. "Colin didn't tell you whether or not I did?"

"He hasn't yet, no. But then I've not texted him to find out. I could, right quick."

"Don't bother. Yes. I filed a report this morning."

There wasn't even a flicker of suspicion in his gaze. He clearly trusted her words. Which he should. She hadn't been blowing smoke up his ass. As much as she'd dreaded it, she'd stopped by the station this morning and Colin had directed her to the right person to file a report with.

"Good. Hopefully something comes of it."

"I have a feeling not much will. He's probably skipped town and is tossing back tequila shots south of the border." She scowled. "With some skanky American tourist giving him a backrub."

"You've spent quite a bit of time considering his current state, I see."

She grunted. "I didn't sleep much last night."

"Sorry to hear that, but I understand." He paused. "If you'd like to leave early tonight, you may."

"Not a chance. I'm not losing another dime." She shook her head, leaving it at that as a customer came to the bar to order.

She resurrected her smile, turned on the friendly attitude and then went and prepared the requested whisky and ginger ale. Five minutes later she'd pocketed a four-dollar tip off the simple drink.

"You bring in more tips than any other bartender here, you realize," Aleck murmured.

"People don't like to be treated like shit. If you treat them nice, smile a little, it goes a long way."

"I don't hire wankers. All my employees are nice. It's more than that. You're personable, you talk to them."

"I enjoy talking to people. Makes my job more fun, plus

you get to know the regulars." She wasn't about to ignore the obvious bit they were both thinking. "But I'm sure the tits and ass part doesn't hurt."

"That's a bit crude."

"Says the man who never fails to appreciate a nice body."

His lips twisted. "You could be ugly as sin and the customers would still flock to you. But, aye, there'll be no denying that you're quite pleasing to the eyes."

"Easy, boss boy. Sexual harassment and all."

"Ah right. Let me rephrase that. You are far more attractive than a Highland cow."

She gave a choked laugh and shook her head. "I think you may have gone from flattery to insults."

"Bah, not at all. Highland cattle are absolutely beautiful, magnificent creatures."

"Really?" she asked skeptically. "And they're different from American cows?"

"Aye. You'll have to Google them."

"I'll get right on that."

He drummed his fingers on the counter. "Did James have any enemies? Or owe anyone any money?"

The deputy at the sheriff's office had asked her the same thing.

"Not that I knew." She hesitated. "I mean, occasionally we'd go to poker parties and he'd throw down some money. But it wasn't all that often."

"Hmm. Casinos?"

"Yes, he'd go to them a couple times a month on his day off. But I don't really think he gambled that much money. I mean, he didn't have a lot to gamble."

"Maybe because he'd gambled it all away previously."

"Look, I don't know what his deal was. What I do know is that my money's gone, and there's a pretty good chance it's not coming back." Tears pricked her eyes and she cursed him for making her nearly cry about this again. She'd cried enough already.

Aleck reached for a bottle of Glenfiddich, poured a shot and handed it to her.

She didn't question it, just accepted the shot, turned her back on the dining room of the pub and downed it. Employees didn't drink often on a shift, but taking a shot now and then wasn't uncommon. Hazards, or perks, of working in a pub.

Besides, who was she to protest when her boss was the one pouring it?

"Better?"

Sure enough, her tears had dried up. "Better. Usually I'm more of a rum girl, but that was good."

"Now get your arse to work. I'm heading to the back to take care of some things."

"Will do."

She watched him disappear. Still upset, but able to appreciate the epic male ass beneath a pair of well-worn jeans.

"I saw that."

Shit. Delonna turned back to the counter and grinned at Kenzie as she sat down on the barstool.

"Saw what?"

"You checking out my brother's backside."

"I was not. I was looking at—" she glanced back the way he'd disappeared "—that puddle of something or other over there."

Kenzie arched a brow and leaned forward to peek over the bar counter.

"That puddle is the size of a quarter. And your eyes were arse level, not floor level."

"I'm not having this conversation."

"It's fine, I'll carry it on for the both of us. You guys really should just sleep together," Kenzie mused. "I've never seen two people more destined to fuck."

She was not the type who blushed easily, but dammit, this was twice in two days she'd had a reason to.

"Why are you here? Aren't you off for the evening?"

"Aye, but I wanted to check on you. And besides that, I'm hungry. Ring in a cheeseburger for me, all right?"

"Done." Delonna typed in the order, knowing her friend well enough to request no onions. "And I'm fine, by the way."

"Are you really? I'm sorry I wasn't home last night. I meant to be, but Brett bought this brilliant wine, and one thing led to another, and—"

"Really, no need to explain. Especially about were it led."

She laughed softly. "I get it, Kenzie. You've got an amazing fiancé you're head over heels in love with. I wouldn't be home either."

"Still, you needed me last night."

"I was fine. And whether I wanted him or not, I had Aleck. Though he was pretty awesome, actually. Even made sure I got home okay."

"Did he now?" Kenzie's eyes brightened. "After he ensured your safety home, did he perhaps sleep over?"

"No. And stop with that line of thought, please."

"Hmm. Bummer."

Delonna gave her a pint of ale and a warning look.

Kenzie sipped the ale, her expression thoughtful. "You realize he canceled a date for you last night?"

Heart stilling, Delonna stared at her friend. "He had a date?"

"Aye. Some customer with too much makeup and a skirt that was about the size of a bandage."

"So his usual type," Delonna muttered.

"So to speak. Or it is when he actually makes an attempt to go on dates, which isn't all that often. Though…never mind."

"Though what?"

Kenzie looked uncomfortable. "It's nothing. It's just that, I suppose *dating* is the wrong word."

Awareness kicked in and Delonna nodded. "Just hooking up?"

"Aye. Probably. Aleck doesn't really date. Hasn't since…" Kenzie closed her mouth and looked away. "He just doesn't anymore."

So Aleck had given up getting laid last night to help her? Why?

The memory of him walking her to the door last night flickered through her head. Of him going in for a kiss. Her heart began to pound harder and her mouth tightened.

"Excuse me for a moment." Glancing around to make sure no customers were going to need immediate help, she strode to the back room.

ALECK HAD JUST begun putting in his whisky orders from their delivery source when Delonna strode into the back. He glanced up, distracted momentarily from the price changes, and glanced at her.

"Everything all right?" He needn't have asked, though, if he went by the compressed lips and warning glint in her eyes.

"Last night, when you showed up to help me. Were you hoping for something in return at the end of the day?"

He stilled, not pleased with what she was implying. Leaning back in his chair, he narrowed his eyes at her.

"As in was I hoping you would shag me?" he asked lightly.

She blinked and then gave a small nod, folding her arms across her chest.

He bit back a snarl of a laugh. Then, as stoically as he could, he rolled his shoulders and said, "Aye."

Her eyes went huge and her body began to tremble. "You complete jerk. You seriously—"

"Bloody hell, no, not seriously." He stood up and rounded the desk toward her.

When she moved to back up, he caught her arm to stop her retreat.

"What kind of fookin' bastart do you take me for?" he demanded.

She didn't try to escape his grasp, but now lifted her chin and met his anger head-on. "Well you had plans to screw someone else, so maybe you figured you'd pull a Boy Scout move with me and get lucky at the same time."

"I helped you last night because I'm a nice guy. I can be one, you realize, when I want to be." He slid his fingers down her arm to join their hands. "And I'm a bit curious as to how you'd know all about my so-called plan to get laid last night."

"Let's just say a little birdie told me."

He glanced at the door behind her, and wagered that if he were to open it he'd find his sister sitting at the bar.

"A little birdie named Kenzie, perhaps?"

"Does it matter?"

"Aye, it does." He pulled her flush against him and this time she did look alarmed. "Because I suspect I don't need to dress up as a knight in shining armor to get you into bed,

Delonna."

She made a little gasp and her eyes went even wider—if that were possible.

"You cocky mother—"

"Your mouth is really much better suited for kissing than cursing, luv."

Before she could finish ripping him a new one, he dipped his head and claimed her lips. It wasn't a need that had begun last night. Not even one from that kiss over the summer. It had been simmering on the back burner from the minute he'd hired her.

When she tried to pull away, he backed her up until she bumped into the closed door. He was completely unwilling to lift his mouth from the softness of hers.

Shite, there was a very good chance he was about to get sued for sexual harassment. Assault. Whatever the hell she wanted to go with if his gamble didn't pay off and she didn't start kissing him back soon.

He teased his tongue against the fullness of her compressed lips and her growl of anger morphed slightly into a moan. Just as quickly, she stopped trying to push him away and instead opened her mouth to him.

Her tongue met his halfway, and instinct and need took over. He gathered her tighter into his arms, deepening the kiss and tasting every inch of her mouth that he'd sampled so briefly last summer.

Completely overwhelmed by the taste and feel of her,

and needing a whole lot more, he slid his hands down her back. Lower and lower still, until they rested on the soft roundness of her arse.

When he kneaded her flesh through the jeans, she made a low groan and rocked forward against him. His cock grew harder as it came into contact with her belly.

He thrust his fingers into her hair, pulling strands free from the ponytail as he held her head still to commandeer her mouth.

Deeper. Slower. Their tongues explored and tasted. She tasted of the whisky shot he'd given her. Sharp and sweet. And it went beyond the alcohol. It was as if he were getting drunk on the kiss. As if he were taking shot after shot.

She twisted her head to the side, and gasped in a breath.

"Lana," he whispered.

Not wanting the break from the sweetness of her, he kissed the side of her mouth. Her jawline. And then the pale curve of her neck exposed over the McLaughlin's Pub V-neck shirt.

She made another low moan and arched into him again. Her head fell back, lifting her full breasts higher and closer to his mouth.

He kissed lower. To the rapidly beating pulse in her neck. Lower still. To the swells of the top of her chest. Her skin was so soft. Addictively sweet like sugar. Christ. He wanted to rip off her top and find out how those gorgeous breasts would feel in his hands. His mouth.

"Customers up front. And my arse isn't working today."

Kenzie's sharp words from the other side of the door were followed by her retreating footsteps.

Son of a bitch. He closed his eyes.

Delonna swore. "Do you think she heard anything?"

"Hmm. Perhaps some heavy breathing. Moans," he said matter-of-factly, and then winced when she slugged his arm. "But then the door is pretty thick, so likely not."

"This is your fault."

"Undeniably." He paused. "Are you going to sue me?"

She was silent for a moment, and then very solemnly said, "Aye."

Throwing it right back at him, was she? His mouth twitched. "I suppose I'd deserve it."

"I suppose you would. But then that'd make me a hypocrite for kissing you back and liking it." She eased back from him, but lightly touched his chest. "Then nearly stripping down and jumping you on your desk."

Statements like that were not going to help his hard-on. He glanced at his desk. "You know, it's not actually too late."

"We're working. And as Kenzie just yelled, there are customers to serve and that sort of thing." She slid out from beneath his arm and began to refasten her mussed ponytail. "Should we just pretend this didn't happen?"

"Again?"

She cast him a sharp look.

"Maybe you could blame it on pain meds once more?" he mocked, irritated that she wanted to sweep it under the rug.

"This shouldn't have happened."

"But it did. And it's happened twice now. And instead of pretending as if it hasn't, maybe we should acknowledge there is a legitimate sexual attraction between us."

"No."

"You're denying you're attracted to me?"

"No." She turned on him, her ponytail swinging now. "I'm not denying anything, Aleck. But you're my boss. Sleeping with you is a big fat *no*. You don't do it."

He paused. "You're fired."

"*What?*"

"Kidding of course. I'll not discipline you for sleeping with me."

She didn't look any less shocked.

"Or, er, not sleeping with me. Either way, there won't be consequences. Is this confusing? It feels a bit confusing." He thrust a hand through his hair and shook his head.

"You shouldn't have kissed me."

"Clearly. But you kissed me the first time during summer."

"What is this, first grade? Besides, I was on pain meds that time."

He gave a lopsided smile. "Aye, by all means, blame the drugs."

The flash of embarrassment in her eyes made him realize the excuse had been as flimsy in her mind as it was in his.

"I, on the other hand, have no excuse," he continued lightly. "I simply wanted to kiss you a moment ago and did so."

"Okay, you need to stop saying stuff like that."

He nodded. "I'll certainly try."

"What do you mean try? There is no *try*!"

"Yoda?"

She looked confused, before shaking her head and darting out of the office.

He sighed. So perhaps *not* a *Star Wars* fan. He went back to his desk, where he knew getting anything done was going to be damn near impossible.

Chapter Five

"MORE WINE?"

When Hailey entered the living room with the wine bottle in hand, Kenzie and Delonna put out their glasses.

"Oh you can definitely top me off. I need it," Delonna murmured as her friend sloshed some more merlot into her glass. She took a sip and appreciated the sweet warmth as it slid down her throat.

"I wish," Sarah chimed in. "I know the doctor said a glass now and then wouldn't hurt while breastfeeding, so it's not that. I just know the wine will knock me out from being so sleep-deprived."

"No worries, we're just glad to have you here," Hailey murmured. "And I'm not drinking either, as usual. I'm just here for the company."

"Me too." Sarah groaned. "I needed this Girls' Night In more than you know."

"You deserve it. Newborns are exhausting." Kenzie took a sip of wine and raised a finger. "Mmm. Which is why I only babysit for a couple of hours at a time."

"I'll take those two hours gratefully, and besides you're fabulous enough to take Emily plenty of times for overnights."

As the discussion turned to Sarah's nearly teen daughter Emily, Delonna looked around the living room. It was amazing that she and Kenzie had somehow gotten it cleaned before it was their turn to host a gathering tonight.

Girls' Night In. It had to be the sixth one of these they'd had in the past year, since they started making it a thing. Wine, cheese and lots of girl talk once a month. It was replenishment for the soul.

"How is my little nephew Ben doing?" Kenzie asked.

"Very sweet and mild," Sarah mused. "He's a pretty easy baby. Clearly, he takes after me. Whereas Emily—"

"Is a dead ringer, personality-wise, for Ian," Hailey finished dryly.

Anyone who knew Ian McLaughlin and Emily could tell right away which parent the girl took after temperamentwise. Physically, while she had the vibrant McLaughlin green eyes, she resembled her mother almost perfectly with her petite height and long, dark hair.

But her penchant for getting into trouble and having little to no filter on her words was so much like her dad. It was amazing more people hadn't realized from the start that Emily was Ian's child. Their whole romantic story sounded straight out of soap opera.

Delonna glanced at the three other women in the room. In the past couple of years they'd all become tight friends. Everyone in this room was either a blood McLaughlin or married to one. And then there was Delonna, who really had no romantic relation to any of the McLaughlins, just friends with them all.

Or no romantic relation until a couple months ago, a voice whispered in her head. And then again on Sunday.

A wave of heat slid through her and she took another sip of her wine, trying to distract herself from the memory of what had happened in Aleck's office. But it was there. Tapping away in her memory like a woodpecker. She'd made out with her boss. Again. And holy shit it had been hot. Had felt so damn good. Why hadn't she stopped him? Son of a biscuit, *why hadn't she stopped him*?

"Delonna?"

Delonna blinked and glanced over at Sarah, who had said her name. "I'm sorry, what?"

"You were spacing out. Are we boring you with the baby talk?" Sarah gave a rueful smile. "I'm sorry, it's kind of my whole reality right now. I'll try not to ramble too much."

"No. I love babies and Ben is adorable. I, just, my mind slipped elsewhere." *Like your brother-in-law.* "Sorry."

"Aye, the stolen money. And how could you not think about it?" Kenzie nodded, her gaze softening.

Stolen money. Right. One would think that would be first and foremost in her mind right now, but hey. Priorities.

"Yeah." She ran with Kenzie's assumption. "It's hard not to think about it."

"I'm so sorry about what happened. Colin mentioned it to me assuming I knew," Hailey said cautiously, referring to her detective hubby.

"It's fine. It's not a secret." Delonna gave a tight smile. "I'm putting out an APB for all my friends if you see James. Permission to kick him in the balls and run."

"I'm in," Hailey agreed. "What did the sheriff's office say they could do for you?"

"They're going to make an effort to find the guy, but it's harder because he lives off the island."

"Wait, wait. I'm lost. Baby brain, my fault." Sarah shook her head. "Who stole your money?"

"James."

Sarah gasped. "As in your boyfriend James?"

"Pretty safe to say they've broken up, aye?" Kenzie asked, shooting Delonna a quick look.

"Stealing six thousand dollars of my money is kind of a deal breaker in a relationship."

Sarah nearly spit out the soda in her mouth. "Holy fucking shit."

For someone who rarely swore, Sarah did so remarkably well when she wanted to.

"Exactly," Delonna agreed, that sinking feeling in her stomach returning.

"I am so sorry, honey."

"Me too." She would not cry again. She wouldn't. After blinking quickly about ten times until the moisture dried up, she took another sip of wine.

"Well. He was kind of a jerk anyway," Sarah murmured.

"Mmm. I thought so too." Hailey nodded.

Kenzie shrugged. "I mean, he was cute. In a rough-and-tough biker kind of way."

Delonna frowned. "Wait, so none of you liked him? And no one said anything?"

She looked around at the guilty expressions.

"Well I mean, he wasn't awful," Sarah explained, "and you seemed into him. So we let you have fun. I mean, clearly he's not the type of guy you marry, but then you're only twenty-four."

More murmurs of agreement and Delonna resisted the urge to roll her eyes. With her friends just starting their thirties, they tended to look at her as the younger party girl. Even if they'd learned by now she'd moved out of those days before even hitting the legal age to drink.

She might not be looking for serious right now, but that didn't mean she was opposed to it if the right guy came along. He'd just have to be *ridiculously* right. Because a husband would be a big distraction from the plans she had.

"Well I hope they find the bastard." Hailey shook her head. "Because that's just awful."

The other women made murmurs of agreement.

"So you've filed a police report. Are single again..." Sarah gave her a thoughtful look. "You know I might know this guy—"

"No." Delonna gave a firm shake of her head. "I'm on a dating hiatus."

Hailey grunted. "Maybe it's for the best."

Delonna felt it then. Kenzie's gaze on her, just as scrutinizing and direct as Aleck's could be. Delonna made the mistake of glancing up and making eye contact with her friend. The little knowing gleam in her eyes meant Kenzie had probably figured out what had happened between Delonna and Aleck on Sunday.

And yet she hadn't said anything about it, though maybe that's because they hadn't had much time alone to chat. Delonna glanced away quickly, hoping the guilt wasn't written all over her face.

"I think the artichoke dip is almost done cooking. Let me go check on that." Looking for any excuse to escape for a moment, Delonna slipped from the room and went to the kitchen.

Her solitude was short-lived though as Kenzie appeared beside her. Averting her eyes, Delonna pulled the bubbling dip from the oven.

"That smells amazing." Kenzie eyed it appreciatively. "Full of all kinds of sinful calories."

"Absolutely."

"Almost as sinful as making out with your boss, I'd imagine."

And there it was. Kenzie wasn't the type to let things go unsaid. Still, it didn't mean Delonna had to confirm them.

"I have no idea what you're talking about."

Kenzie just arched a brow in the same aggravating manner that Aleck did.

"I mean, did you see something?" Delonna asked innocently as she grabbed a bag of tortilla chips and dumped them into a bowl. "Hear something?"

"It was what I didn't hear that gave it away. You two were far too quiet in there."

"Those doors are thick. I'm sure you just didn't hear us talking."

"Not that thick, and the way you stormed off I assumed there'd be a brilliant screaming match." Kenzie plucked a chip from the bowl and took a bite of it.

"I didn't storm off."

"Aye, you certainly did. You were livid. But about what? That he abandoned a date for you?"

"No, I just..." Made a really stupid assumption, and had confronted him about it. Just thinking about it made mortification slide through her.

"I'm hardly going to judge you for getting involved with Aleck. I actually encouraged it in good fun—"

"We're not involved."

"But I should also warn you to be careful," Kenzie continued, gentling her tone. "I don't want to see you get hurt. Especially so soon after James."

"Kenz." Delonna struggled to find a reply, but realized her friend wasn't going to waver on what she believed. "Fine. Yes, there was a moment of heavy kissing. Whatever. But that doesn't really add up to me getting hurt or us even being involved. It was a mistake, and it won't happen again."

"It will." Kenzie looked grave as she grabbed another chip. "You've broken the seal and there's no going back now. May as well just screw and get it over with."

"Which is basically what you've been saying from the start. So why the concern now?"

"Because I never thought you guys would take me seriously, and now my conscience has kicked in. I know how Aleck is with women."

"I do too. I'm not under any illusions that he's looking to settle down anytime soon, Kenz."

"Good."

"Is that dip ready?" Sarah hollered from the living room. "Some of us are eating as if we were still pregnant."

Delonna and Kenzie shared a laugh and moved away from the kitchen.

"And a kiss isn't serious," Delonna said softly again.

Kenzie gave a small sigh. "Is a kiss ever harmless? It's the gateway to so much more. To potentially have amazing sex. Not that I'm trying to envision you and my brother having amazing sex. Let alone sex at all."

"You know, this conversation is pretty sucky."

"Aye, it is. All, I'm saying is, just...be careful."

As her friend moved past her back into the living room, Delonna felt a slither of unease race through her.

For a moment she let herself briefly imagine hitting the accelerator instead of the brakes with Aleck. The way her pulse quickened and her body heated, she couldn't deny it sounded all too appealing.

And a little concerning.

"HOW'S DELONNA HOLDING up?"

Aleck glanced up from where he was arranging the bottles of alcohol.

"She's all right. Thanks for helping her file the police report."

Colin nodded. "Aye, well she should've come to the station in the first place."

"She was just worried, having not reported the tips and all. Where's Hailey tonight?"

"Girls' Night In over at Kenzie's and Delonna's. I'm surprised the ladies didn't mention it."

"Me too," he mused. "Then again it's Kenzie's day off and Delonna worked the day shift. Who all goes?"

"The whole lot of them. Sarah, Hailey, Delonna and Kenzie."

"Did Sarah bring the baby?"

"Not tonight. I dropped by Ian's earlier and he and Emily were on the floor playing with the wee one. Tummy time or something of the sort."

"He's taken naturally to having an infant about. And he's remarkably good with Emily as well." Aleck shook his head.

And to think Ian had been the one they'd all said would never have children. Now he had two and was a natural at being a father.

"Aye. He's doing quite well."

"What about you and Hailey?" Aleck slid his brother another beer. "Starting a family soon?"

"Actually, aye, we've been trying."

Not having expected that answer, Aleck gave a slow nod. Though why he was surprised, he couldn't say. Maybe Hailey and Colin had only been married for a handful of months, but they were both just past thirty and clearly in the mind to become parents.

"Good. I'll enjoy another niece or nephew."

"And you?" Colin lifted an eyebrow. "Are you not getting the itch to settle down and have a family of your own?"

Any amusement faded and Aleck gave a brisk shake of his head. "I'm not the marrying sort."

"It's funny, because I sensed you once were."

He glanced up sharply at his brother's soft words. Aleck's blood quickened and he gave a small shake of his head.

"That was another lifetime. I was a different man then."

"You weren't even a man, Aleck. More a boy."

"I was seventeen. That's hardly a child in nappies."

"Maybe not, but it was nearly two decades ago.

Shouldn't you open yourself up to the possibility—"

"I'm happy with my life," Aleck interrupted curtly. "I enjoy women on a certain level. A fun, physical level. Perhaps even a friendship level."

"That's a shallow place to exist with women. You should try deeper waters."

"I have."

"Try again. Love isn't a one-shot deal in life, Aleck."

"A matter of opinion. I'd rather not try to find out otherwise." He'd rather stick a hot poker through his foot than go through that kind of pain again. "Spouses and wee ones may be in the cards for the rest of you, but it became evident that it was not my future."

"What about Delonna?"

Aleck stilled and arched a brow at his brother. "What about her?"

"You two have a thing going yet?"

Yet? Apparently it was common theory that even if they didn't they soon would.

"Delonna is an employee at the pub, and a friend at best. There's nothing more there."

"No?" Amusement flickered across Colin's face. "All right then. I'll let it drop for now."

He'd damn well better. Aleck had a difficult time as it was trying not to think about what had happened between him and Delonna in the office. Now his younger brother was going to poke fun at him?

There was no point dwelling on it. Delonna had shut that door to their attraction as quickly as he'd opened it. But she was right. Best forget it had ever happened.

"Hey, so you talk to Da lately?" Colin asked randomly.

"Aye, late last night. Called and spoke to him and Ma."

"I called in the morning Sunday. He didn't sound quite right, did you notice?"

"Aye." Aleck frowned, unsettled that his brother had noticed the same thing. "I'd assumed he was tired because I woke him, but he seemed distracted. Come to think of it, Ma did most of the talking."

"That's what I noticed."

"Not completely uncommon."

"No, a bit normal," Colin agreed with a small laugh. "But still."

"Still. I'll call them later and make sure everything's all right."

"Good." Colin pulled out his phone that had vibrated and glanced down. "And this would be Hailey, ready to be picked up from Girls' Night it seems. I should head out."

When his brother went to hand him money, Aleck waved it away. "You ought to know better by now. Give Hailey a kiss for me."

"Aye, on the cheek. Her lips are mine." Colin winked and turned away, calling out, "Thanks for the beer, Brother."

After Colin had left the pub, Aleck turned his attention back to work. CJ was holding down the bar, and Theresa and Betty were working the floor.

It was slow enough he could potentially offer Betty the opportunity to go home early.

Unfortunately, he really shouldn't send himself home, though the idea was tempting. Not that he had anywhere exciting to be. He'd killed any chance at getting laid with Melissa. Not that he really regretted it. It would've just been a couple nights of fun and then likely nothing else.

It was getting tiring. Boring. Colin's words floated back to him, that maybe he'd want more.

No. He'd had more, and in the end it had given him nothing but regret and pain. Maybe it was a shallow existence, but the deep end of the romance pool was forever off limits to him.

Aleck set his jaw and went out to the floor to find Betty and offer her the choice to go home.

~

"YOU'RE SURE YOU'RE okay with this?"

Delonna gave Kenzie a look of disbelief. Sarah and Hailey had gone home an hour ago, and Kenzie's man Brett had showed up to drop something off but had ended up staying.

"I'm fine. I promise I have no issue with Brett staying the night. You crash at his place enough—I'm sure he appreciates you returning the favor. Seriously, Kenz, don't sweat it. The walls are thick. I won't hear anything."

Kenzie turned slightly pink, even as she rolled her eyes.

"Even if we do that we'll keep it down." She glanced down the hall. "Or I could just join him in the shower, right quick."

"Now that sounds like an excellent idea."

Half joking, she laughed as Kenzie nodded and made her way to the bathroom. She winked at Delonna, before slipping through the door.

A small pang of jealousy swept through her. Not necessarily at the sex her friend was about to have, but just that Kenzie had found someone she was so absolutely in love with.

Love. She wanted it some day. The romance. The husband and babies. But right now she was married to her future. Still, the idea of having someone was nice.

After making her way back to her room, Delonna grabbed a small folder from inside her dresser. From it she pulled out her five-year plan and sighed. It was going to look more like seven years with the way things were going.

She closed the folder and leaned back on her bed, staring at the ceiling. She'd just have to rebuild her savings, and this time in an actual savings account. It had been stupid to hoard that kind of money in a coffee bin, no matter her reasons.

The sharp pealing of the doorbell had her glancing to the hallway with a frown.

It was nearly midnight. Who was that?

Grabbing the baseball bat she kept in her closet, she

made her way to the front door. A quick glance through the peephole showed no one outside anymore, but a bouquet of flowers on the porch.

Interesting. They were probably not for Kenzie since her man was currently in the shower with her. Had Aleck sent them?

Leaning the bat against the wall, she unlocked the door and then the dead bolt. She swung it open a moment later and took a step out to retrieve the bouquet.

The hand that wrapped around her throat cut off her shocked gasp. She was shoved back against the door so hard she saw stars. In the dark she could barely see the shadowed gaze that peered at her through the ski mask.

"You tell your boyfriend I want the rest of my money," a voice rasped. "Fifteen hundred isn't going to cut it."

She tried to choke out a reply, but he'd literally cut off her air supply with his gloved hands. Breathing was her number one goal, even as fear roared through her.

She clawed at his hand to try to free herself, but his grip didn't ease a bit.

"He has until the end of the week. Next time I'm not going to be so polite while asking for my money."

This was polite?

Her head began to feel light and her vision blurred. Then she was free. Crumbling to a hump on the porch and dragging in air as he ran off into the night.

Crawling to the door, she grabbed the handle and twisted, before falling inside with a ragged cry. The shower was still running, though, and she knew they wouldn't hear her. She stumbled to her feet, the terror still so sharp she shook from it.

Tears blurred her eyes and she touched her sore neck, knowing there'd probably be red marks if she looked in the mirror.

Fuck. James clearly owed someone money, and whoever the violent ass-clown was, he had just decided to come after her.

She knew why. Because he couldn't find James either.

The shower turned off and a few minutes later the door swung open. Luckily Kenzie glanced her way and saw her crumpled on the floor.

"What the hell?" Kenzie rushed forward, tightening the towel around her body. "What happened?"

God. She didn't want to do this. She *really* didn't want to do this. "Can you…dammit. Can you call the police?"

"Aye." Kenzie's eyes sharpened with realization and shock. "Brett, I need you. *Now*!"

Chapter Six

DELONNA WAS JUST finishing up giving the officer her statement when there was another sharp knock on the door.

Kenzie caught her eye and waved as she made to stand. "I'll get that, it's probably one of my other brothers."

Another one? Colin had already showed up along with the sheriff's deputy. How that had even happened, who knew? He wasn't even on shift.

Maybe because Kenzie had been the one to place the call and the McLaughlin men were probably kept apprised on everything that went on with their sister.

"What the bloody hell happened?"

Delonna cringed, recognizing Aleck's voice before he even rounded the corner. Another brother was right. The deputy raised an eyebrow at his arrival, but continued making notes. Maybe Aleck was no stranger to him either.

When Aleck entered the room, his gaze immediately sought her out. His eyes were bright with concern as he slid his gaze over her from top to bottom.

A tremor ran through her, and it had nothing to do with fear this time.

"Lana?" His tone sharpened.

"It's over now," she said quietly. "We're fine, Aleck."

"That's not what I asked." He strode toward her and crouched down where she sat in a chair. He missed nothing as his focus turned to her neck. "What happened?"

Her pulse quickened because she knew he'd seen the faint bruises there. His mouth became a grim slash and he shook his head. "You were attacked?"

Like she could deny it. "Yeah. And how does word travel so fast on this island?"

He ignored the question. "Any idea who the bastart was?"

"I think this guy here is actually doing the questioning." She gestured to the deputy, who just made a small grunt of amusement, but didn't look up.

Aleck glanced at his sister. "It's not safe here. You'll be staying at Brett's house tonight?"

Brett, who stood close to Kenzie, gave a nod. "With the new circumstances, yes, sir, Kenzie will be coming home with me now. And I have an extra room for Delonna—"

"No," Delonna cut in. "Thank you for the offer, Brett, but you don't need to take me in. I'll be fine."

"You'll be fine," Aleck said, "because you'll be staying with me."

Her heart full-on lurched now at how nonnegotiable his

statement had been. Then lurched again at the idea of actually staying under his roof.

Absently, she shook her head. "I don't...no. No I'm not."

"Aye, you are." He strode out of the room and she opened her mouth to argue with him again, but the deputy asked her another question and distracted her.

A few minutes later she was signing off on something and seeing the deputy out. Unfortunately he *also* recommended having someone either stay the night or that she consider staying elsewhere. The word "elsewhere" being spoken with a pointed glance to where Aleck had disappeared down the hall.

Clearly he was team Aleck.

After the deputy had left, and Kenzie and Brett were watching her with matching concerned expressions, Delonna sighed.

"It's fine, guys. You're probably better off going to Brett's, just in case."

"So you'll stay at Aleck's then?" Kenzie prodded. "Because we'll not leave otherwise."

Crap. "Sure. Yeah, I'll go there."

Not a chance. She wasn't letting some intimidating asshole drive her out of her home.

"Good." Aleck reappeared. "I've packed you an overnight bag."

She stilled, even as her blood pressure spiked. "I'm sorry,

you did what?"

"Ah shit," Kenzie muttered. "We'd best go, Brett. There's no help for it now."

Delonna barely noticed them leaving, she was so intent at staring Aleck down.

"I think you just crossed a line," she finally managed. "I'm not really okay with you pawing through my underwear drawer."

"Purely clinical mode as I did so, I assure you. Though I was partial to the tiny white knickers with the pink stars so I put them in there. Anyway, shall—"

"No, we shall not *anything*. I'm not going with you." If anything, she was about to punch him in the stomach. The idea of him handling her panties was enough to make her current ones get in a bunch.

"Not going with me?" He watched her for a moment, and then nodded. "Fine. I'll stay here then."

He dropped the bag with her stuff on the floor. Her teeth snapped together.

"Look, before you try and rip me a new one," he said gently, "just answer me this. Would you feel safe alone here tonight? And the truth, Lana."

Just like that her anger died. No. She wouldn't. She'd be in fear all night of her attacker returning, intent on further threats or harm. Aleck must've seen the answer on her face because he made a small grunt of awareness.

"I see. Then make your choice."

For a moment she was tempted to tell him to crash here, because the idea of going with him and being at his house was a little overwhelming. For more than one reason.

She let her gaze drift around the house, before settling on the door. The image of being attacked on the front porch flitted through her head and an icy chill slid down her back.

Whoever was looking for James knew where she lived and seemed to be holding her equally accountable. She wasn't safe here, no matter how much she wanted to believe otherwise. He'd said she had a week, but what if he changed his mind? Wanted to up his threat a little?

"If you're sure—" she swallowed her pride "—then I'd like to go to your place. And please don't take that as a come-on, because I'm too damn tired to flirt."

"Understandable. I'll treat you as I would my sister tonight, I swear it," he murmured solemnly. "Come. Lock up and we'll be on our way."

THINKING OF DELONNA as a sister was much easier said than done. Not that she was being suggestive or sexual around him. Quite the opposite.

She was curled up in his recliner, legs bare below the pink boxer shorts. The gray sweatshirt she wore was oversized and fell off one shoulder.

Her hair was in a messy bun-type thing on top of her head, and her hands were wrapped around a steaming cup of hot chocolate. Her nails were still decorated with chipped blue polish, which she'd painted last Sunday for the Seahawks game.

When she pursed her lips and blew on the hot chocolate, the blood in his veins heated. There was something so damn down to earth and sensual about her. He wanted to take the mug from her hands and then pull each article of clothing from her body.

What fascinated him most at this moment were her legs, long and pale, so completely on display. It was nearing November and chilly as fook. Shouldn't she be wearing long fleece pajamas or something of the sort?

"I like your place," she murmured, glancing around over the top of her mug. "How long have you owned it?"

"My parents bought it when they moved here from Edinburgh and we all lived here at some time or another. When they moved back to Scotland, they sold me the house for a very decent price, with the understanding that it'd be a home to my siblings should they need or want it."

As her brows drew together and he saw the question brewing on her lips, he continued. "And it's not something I resented or felt blackmailed into. I love my family. Love my brothers and sister. Our parents. We're all quite close, and as you know, Kenzie lived here until she moved into your house."

"Well, not really mine. I rent. But yes, I remember that. I thought it was...kind of sweet really. How protective you were of her. How you all still are."

"We've every right to be. Trouble has always found a way of following Kenzie."

Kenzie's past included being nearly raped. Twice, actually, and by the same guy. Fortunately, he was behind bars now.

"You're going to have to ease up on that overly protective brother stuff, though," Delonna teased. "She's got an equally loving protector now."

"Aye. I quite like Brett. I think he's a perfect match for Kenzie, and I completely trust her in his hands."

"It's fascinating seeing you McLaughlin guys with the women in your lives. Whether it's your sister, or your girlfriends, or your wives. Like there's nothing you wouldn't do for them."

"And there's not," he agreed.

"It has a very Highlander feel—sorry, generalizing here, I'm sure—just very old-fashioned and primitive."

"Highlander?" Amusement pricked through him. "You're referencing my ancestors now, aye?"

"What can I say? Ever since I saw you in that kilt for the bachelor auction, it's hard to get that image out of my head."

She said the words lightly enough, but there was a gleam in her eyes that made him think there was some truth to her words.

"And why should you? I look quite decent in a kilt," he teased.

She laughed and rolled her eyes. "And you're not at all humble about it."

"Not even a little bit. You ever been to Scotland, lass?"

"Lass? Breaking out all the Scottish words. Careful, you're risking getting me all hot and bothered."

She was full-on flirting now. Often harmless, but when she was underdressed sitting in his house late at night, a bit more chancy.

"Och." He lowered his voice an octave, knowing the female response to the deep bass tone. "You donna say."

Her laugh was breathy this time and she shifted in the seat, sliding her gaze away. "Oh *aye*."

The distance between the chair and couch seemed like yards, rather than feet now. The urge to walk over, scoop her up and carry her back to the couch and his lap was hitting strong.

"And, no," she continued, somewhat tartly, "I've never been to Scotland. And I doubt I ever will because it'd be so damn pricey. Have you seen how much airfare costs?"

"Aye." He nodded. "I've gotten quite good at spotting the deals."

A wistful smile crossed her face. "I'd like to go. I'm just…pretty stingy with my money."

"A Scot at heart."

"Absolutely." She lifted the hot chocolate to her lips to take another sip but yawned instead. "Oh man, I should just go to bed. I'm exhausted and probably will be crappy company soon, if I'm not already."

"You're charming company." And she was. The idea of her heading off to bed already disappointed a bit, but he couldn't blame her for wanting sleep. "You remember where the room is?"

"Pretty sure I can find it."

"It's just one room down from mine."

Her gaze flitted to his over the rim of her mug, and he saw the consideration in her eyes. As if she were contemplating maybe not going to bed after all. Or not alone, that was.

Or maybe that's just wishful thinking.

She set her mug down and walked over to him. His heart began a slow thud and the blood in his veins rushed south. When she stood over him and then leaned down slightly to brush her lips over his, his cock leapt in anticipation.

But before he could appreciate the softness of her mouth, or the hint of her perfume, she'd lifted her head and stepped back.

"Thank you for letting me crash here," she said softly. "You really are a nice guy, boss boy."

And then she was gone in a blur of bare legs.

Shite.

He let his breath hiss from between clenched teeth. That little kiss had done nothing but get his body and mind more excited. And then she'd walked away. But when he weighed the possibility of not having had the kiss or having it with a lasting hard-on now, he chose the latter.

He'd have Lana in his bed. Maybe not tonight, maybe not tomorrow, or even in the weeks to come. But they *would* sleep together. The sexual tension between them swelled more each day, and he knew she was equally aware of it. Fought it.

He suspected them ending up in bed together was as inevitable as rain in Seattle. And when he thought about it, he could acknowledge that really, she was the perfect person to get involved with.

Delonna was confident with her body and sexuality. She was quite young still, not even twenty-five, and just out of a relationship. She wouldn't be looking for anything serious. Which was perfect for him.

Standing up to turn off the lights, he tried not to think about what it'd be like having her beneath him. Being inside her. Having those amazing breasts in his hands. His mouth.

Fook.

Going to sleep was going to have to wait a bit for him. First on the agenda was a cold shower.

~

"YOU THINK MAYBE I should go home tonight?" As Delonna asked the question, she pretty much knew what his answer would be. The irritation and dismay that flashed across Aleck's face just confirmed he thought it silly.

"Let's err on the side of caution and keep you at my place for at least a bit longer."

She nodded, and didn't bother to hide her sigh. The night was winding down and the pub closed in less than an hour. They'd carpooled to work, which made her question equally ridiculous. Still, she hated being dependent on anyone, or feeling like she was imposing her presence on someone.

"I realize it's inconvenient." He moved past her to rearrange several bottles of hard alcohol. "And you'd rather not be stuck staying with me, but I'm concerned—"

"It's not that." She shook her head. "It's just that it's your house, and I'm sure my being there makes it a little hard if you wanted to bring someone..." She broke off, wishing she hadn't gone down that road.

"Bring someone home?" He arched a brow. "Truly? You think I'm entertaining the idea of bringing another woman home with me?"

"Well, you're a guy." It sounded a lot lamer aloud than it had in her head.

"Ah, so that means I should want to bury my cock in any available hole at all possible times?"

She choked and shot a glance around the pub, glad most of the people had already left for the night and no one had heard him.

"Well, if you want to be crude about it." The words *had* been crude, but said with a tone of amusement. Unfortunately, her mind had put visuals to his statement, and it made something hot slide through her blood.

"Really. 'You're a guy.' That's such a completely shite statement, and really, Lana, I expected better from you."

She huffed out a breath. "Look. You're a very attractive man, who, from what I've seen, has never had a problem attracting female attention. I don't want to put a kink in your love life."

"Thank you, on the first part. But answer me this. Do you see me leaving with these females?"

Why had she started this conversation again? She hesitated. "Well, no. But maybe you arrange meetings later—"

"I don't." His jaw flexed. "And you should just stop while you're ahead, lass."

Being called "lass" made her feel like she was about eight years old and he was talking to a child. But then, the glare he directed at her now was a pretty good indication he thought this conversation was childish. And it probably was.

"I just wanted to make sure. My life is already on hold, and I hate the idea that I'm interrupting yours too," she finished lamely.

He abandoned whatever task he'd been doing with the alcohol and closed the distance between them. She was already against the back counter and had nowhere to move but to the side, but she held her place.

"I don't need to shag constantly like some randy college boy, Lana. Aye, I love sex—what man doesn't?" His hands closed over the counter on either side of her body. "But right now I'm holding out for one woman in particular."

The hair on the back of her neck lifted and her pulse quickened. "Are you now?"

"Aye. She's a stunner. Cheeky. Confident." His head dipped so his lips were near her ear. "Has an incredible arse I keep imagining in my hands."

The blood in her veins turned to liquid heat and she closed her eyes momentarily. His breath was warm against her ear, and even though they weren't touching, she was utterly aware of his tall, broad-shouldered body just inches from hers.

"This is so inappropriate," she muttered raggedly. "You're my boss."

"Aye. We've discussed this, and no doubt I should leave you be. Say the word, and I'll treat you as I would my sister."

As uncertain as she was about getting involved with Aleck, the idea of a platonic relationship was more disappointing.

She gave a shaky laugh. "Well now you're just talking nonsense."

"Agreed." He pulled back enough to stare down at her. "I'll not rush you, Lana. When you're ready, my bed will be waiting."

He was so unapologetically blunt. It was both sexy as hell and aggravating.

"I want to," she admitted, her voice low. "You know I do. But you've gotta realize I'm kind of a mess with my last relationship having ended abruptly with all kinds of drama."

"I know. And let me repeat: I'll not rush you. I'll leave the ball in your court." He touched her cheek, lightly, before moving away.

Just in time, as the customer who'd been playing pool in the next room arrived at the bar.

"It's getting mighty windy out there." Old Man Cooper, a regular, dropped a twenty on the bar and shook his head. "My wife keeps texting me to come home—she's a nag, all right. Guess there's some trees down already. You kids be careful when you get out of here."

Delonna gave a small smile. "I love how he always refers to his wife as a nag."

"Aye, he does. But it's all in a bit of fun. She's a nice lady, who doesn't come in much. But they've been married fifty-five years and are happy as can be." Aleck gave the bar counter a smack. "Right then. I'll be in the back if you need me."

Delonna watched him disappear into the office portion down the hall near the bathrooms, and pressed a hand to her cheek. He'd only just touched her lightly, and still her body had responded.

When they finally locked up the pub and left to go back to his place, it became clear the windstorm was no light breeze. The hood of her sweatshirt was thrust off her head from a gust of wind, and it took serious momentum to walk against it and get to his truck.

Inside, the vehicle shook from the large gusts and she

flinched each time it did.

"Blowy as fook out here," Aleck muttered, starting the car. "Hope there're no trees down on the way home."

There weren't any, fortunately, and she knew his house had none directly in its path either. So they were safe from any fear of branches falling once they got there. It was the drive that would be the dangerous part.

She watched the tall trees bending and waving in the wind, and a shiver of fear slid through her. Windstorms had always been a little terrifying, especially on this part of the island. Oak Harbor wasn't really protected from the strong winds that could rush in off the straits.

When they reached his home she could see the waves crashing violently onto the large rocks nearby. They climbed out of the car and made a dash for it.

Once inside the house, Aleck locked the door behind him and rubbed his hands together.

"Quite cold out there, aye? Would you like some tea with a bit of whisky in it?"

"That would be great. But just a splash of whisky, please. I don't sleep well if I've had too much. Which is backward, I know."

"Understood. Go make yourself comfy on the couch, find us a show and I'll bring it out in a few."

Chapter Seven

WHILE WAITING FOR the teapot to boil, Aleck went to turn up the heat a couple degrees to overheat the house a bit. There was a good chance they'd lose power tonight, and it would be better to have a surplus of heat to dwindle from when that happened.

When he brought the two steaming mugs to the living room minutes later, he found Delonna sitting on the couch, legs curled under her, with a blanket on her lap. She'd turned on some sort of thriller flick it appeared.

He joined her after handing her the mug. She scooted over slightly and pulled the blanket toward him.

"Here, have part of this—I'm easy."

"Clearly you're *not* all that easy," he drawled, unable to help himself. He was rewarded with her elbow in his ribs and he laughed.

They fell into a comfortable silence, watching the movie and sharing a blanket, but not quite touching. He itched with the need to close those couple inches between them. To feel her hip brush against his.

It was nice having someone on the same internal clock as him. Not getting off work 'til the wee small hours of the morning meant it took an hour or two to unwind before he fell asleep. Which also meant he slept in longer than most people. All in all it had been a tricky thing when bringing women home. Which was one reason he really hadn't, and had preferred to go their place and slip out before dawn.

But it had been several months now since he'd been in that situation or even had a woman, and with Delonna's soft, perfumed body so close to him, his cock was once again reminded of the fact.

Yet somehow, through the entire movie and the wind gusts shaking the house, he kept himself from touching her. He'd told her the ball was in her court, and hadn't lied.

Her hand on his leg had him jerking in anticipation, but her accompanying words disappointed.

"I'm going to head to bed. Thanks for the whisky and company." She hesitated, then brushed a kiss against his cheek.

Unable to stop himself, he caught the back of her neck and pulled her head back down. It was a short and sweet kiss. But it was a chance for him to touch her lips with his own again. To taste the hint of Earl Grey and whisky, and to hear her soft sigh of pleasure. But with a willpower he himself could never summon, Delonna pulled back and stood up.

"Good night, boss boy," she said softly.

His lips twitched into a half smile. "G' night, Lana."

And then she was gone, soft feet padding down the hall before the door to her bedroom clicked shut.

He finished his tea, grabbed their mugs and placed them in the sink, and went to bed himself.

~

THE BUZZING OF his phone woke him up. Disoriented, he managed to surmise that the room was in complete darkness, and the light from the bathroom that usually shone under his door was missing.

It sank in that the power must've just gone out and his cell had buzzed as it stopped charging. Still in a groggy haze, he reached for his cell and glanced at the time. Nearly four thirty in the morning.

Closing his eyes again, he willed himself to fall back asleep. Another massive gust of wind rattled the windows and the house shook slightly. The sound of waves slamming into the beach accompanied the soundtrack of the storm.

It relaxed him, and kept him awake for a bit, because he loved a good windstorm.

The faint knock had his eyes opening and his brows drawing together. Had that come from outside his room or perhaps something against the side of the house?

When he took too long to decide, the door swung open and Delonna stepped into his room.

He sat up, his frown deepening. "Everything all right?"

She didn't answer, but just darted across the room and

climbed into his bed. Her bare feet were cold from the floorboards, brushing against his leg as he scooted over to make room for her.

"I hate storms. It's stupid. I know it makes me a wimp," she rambled quickly.

"No, not at all, luv. It's fine."

"It's not fine, it's embarrassing." She shook her head. "I was eight when there was a bad windstorm, and a tree smashed through my bedroom. It missed my bed by just a foot."

Shock pricked. "*Shite.* I'm sorry, luv. Thank God it missed you. With that happening, I'm surprised you don't have a raving phobia of storms now."

"I don't really. Only now and then, when it's particularly bad. Then the fear can flare up a little. Like it has tonight."

He pulled her closed, stroking a comforting arm down her back, and ready to let her go if she tried to pull away. But she snuggled closer, pressing her palm to his chest and her cheek to his shoulder.

"Thank you." It was almost a whisper, but he'd heard it.

He turned his head to kiss her forehead lightly and her body relaxed even more against his.

"There are no trees to fall on my house," he reassured her. "Just a few waves that might make it onto my porch."

"I know."

Another gust of wind rattled the house and he sensed her flinch in the darkness.

"Tell me something else about your childhood."

In the darkness, he could sense her frowning. "My childhood was all right, but stressful moneywise."

"Moneywise? You were a child, why even concern yourself with such things?"

She gave a short laugh. "Kind of hard not to when your house is foreclosed on and you're essentially homeless."

"Seriously? I'm sorry, Lana. How old were you?"

"Sixteen. Don't sound so worried, we weren't on the streets or anything." She paused. "Well, I mean there were a few nights we slept in the minivan, but mostly we found places to crash."

"With relatives?"

"We didn't have a lot of relatives around here. The aunt we had was in a one-bedroom apartment. She took my younger brother in, but I had to figure out my own thing."

Figure out her own thing? At sixteen? How in the fook…?

"My parents would sleep in the van quite a bit, but I'd try and find friends with couches to crash on for a week or two." She gave a small shrug. "I had to lie, though. Say my parents were traveling or something. It was just too embarrassing."

"How did it happen?" He needed to understand. Couldn't fathom the image she painted. "Did your da lose his job?"

"Yeah, they both did when the recession hit. My parents

weren't big on saving, but were fantastic at spending. They blew their paychecks on things like expensive electronics and new cars they couldn't afford."

"Jesus. I'm sorry, Lana. It's not something a child—and you were still a bloody child—should've had to face."

"You'd be surprised how common it actually is." She adjusted herself in his arms, tracing a finger over his naked chest.

"Clearly I need educating," he murmured, more than a little disturbed at how his vision of whom the homeless were could be so narrow and ignorant.

"But I got through it okay. After about a year of being technically homeless, Dad got a job again. It didn't pay nearly what he'd made before, but it was enough to get us into a cheap apartment. A year later, I was eighteen and moved out on my own. And now my parents are once again making good money, still blowing through it like it grows on trees."

"They haven't learned at all," he murmured. "But you've been doing quite well on your own, from what I've seen."

"Thank you. I try." She paused. "It's why I'm so stingy with my money, you know. Why I like to have cash on the side. The experience…the fear and humiliation, really hammered in that I never want to end up in that kind of situation again."

"Completely understandable, and I'm so glad you've landed on your feet. You're a smart kid, Lana."

That earned him a light slap on the chest. "*Not* a kid. I already get enough remarks on my age from the gals. Not you too, please."

He grimaced. "Ah, right. I meant it fondly. But consider me properly chastised and a lesson now learned."

A gust of wind started, gaining speed and strength as it began to shake the house. The hardest gust all night. She tensed in his arms, only relaxing when it stopped.

"It's late. You should go back to sleep," he murmured. "I'll hold you as long as you'd like."

"I haven't slept yet."

He blinked in dismay. "Not at all?"

"No. I was wide awake and listening. I have a hard time sleeping through windstorms," she said mildly, her leg tangling with his and her toes sliding over his calf.

His heart quickened.

"There was something about being woken up from a dead sleep when that tree hit my bedroom. I'm afraid, even now, to fall asleep when the wind is this bad. Even knowing there are no trees that could hit your house, my mind doesn't rationalize."

"I understand." And he did. The sympathy he had for her made him press another kiss to her forehead, and keep running his hand lightly up and down her back in a gentle caress. "Just lie here then. Try and at least close your eyes."

"What if I decided I didn't want to just lie here and be held?"

"Then I'd let you go." Reluctantly. Christ, but she felt a bit perfect in his arms. He liked having her here.

"No, I mean, you don't necessarily have to let me go." She paused, tracing his bare chest with a finger again. "You could maybe just...adjust a bit so I can seduce you."

He blinked, his cock going rock hard. What? He doubted he'd heard her right, even as he knew she realized exactly what she'd said.

"Lana, there's no seduction necessary," he said, his voice a bit ragged, as her hand began to travel south down his body.

"No?"

"But I'm happy just to hold you."

"Well, you said the ball was in my court, and this could be a good distraction for me tonight."

Did he want her when she was only looking to him as a distraction?

"I want this." She sat up slightly so she could brush her lips over his nipple. "I've wanted this for a while now."

Aye, hell yes he wanted this. Whether he was a distraction or not. When she kissed his nipple again a shudder of pleasure raced through him. Her hand had reached its destination, cupping him through his boxers as she explored his thickness and length. He nearly came on the spot.

"Maybe we should get you out of these." She slid her hand beneath the shorts and he hissed out a breath. She paused, and even in the darkness he could sense her frown.

"Oh God, talk about corn-fed. You're huge, Aleck."

His laughter was strangled as he took charge and flipped her onto her back.

"If you keep touching me, I'll likely last only minutes," he rasped. "And right now, I've the mind to get in some exploration of my own."

He pulled off the T-shirt she wore and groaned in appreciation as her breasts spilled free for his hands. He cupped them, discovering their firmness and teasing the nipples.

When she let out a sharp moan, he claimed it with his mouth. He wanted to taste her pleasure, and he drove his tongue past her lips as his body covered hers. Her arms eased around his neck and she kissed him back fervently, sucking on his tongue as her hips lifted against him in a silent plea. One he knew exactly how to answer.

He moved his hands beneath her arse, cupped the wonderful roundness there, before tugging the shorts and panties from her body. Sliding a palm between her legs, he rubbed the soft, damp mound of her sex, while tasting every inch of her mouth.

Her legs parted farther and she made a low, needy groan. He knew what she wanted—what he wanted—and slid a finger into her already slick channel.

She cried out, her nails digging into his shoulders. God, she felt incredible. So warm and already wet. He added another finger, stroking her deeper, until he could no longer resist taking it further.

He eased down her body, kissing her breasts and belly button, and finally the plump mound of her sex. She went still, seeming to not even breathe as he nuzzled the damp folds.

"Aleck," she whispered, plunging her hands into his hair and lifting her hips. "Please."

After a soft laugh, he parted the delicate flesh and eased his tongue in to find the spot guaranteed to set her on fire. Her sharp cry and the sensual taste of her only drove up his need to please her. To completely claim her in this way.

He teased her with his tongue. Sucking and flicking, all the while pressing a finger into her tight sheath.

All too soon her moans turned guttural and her body began to quake. She lifted her hips from the bed, crying out and digging her heels into the mattress.

Following her through the orgasm, he gentled his deliberate strokes. He switched to small, delicate kisses on her swollen clit as she let out a shuddering breath and her body went limp.

"Holy shit, boss boy," she muttered, her words thick and drowsy. "I'm beginning to understand why the ladies love you McLaughlin men. Something in the water where you guys grew up in Scotland?"

"Oh, aye." He laughed, pressing a kiss to her inner thigh. "Shall I stop there, luv?"

"Don't you dare," she murmured drowsily. "I'm looking for a home run tonight."

"Quaint little term you Yanks are ever so fond of," he drawled. "But I'm happy to oblige."

And he was, what with a needy erection and a willing and ready woman in his bed.

"I'll just grab a condom right quick." He eased away from her, stumbling in the dark toward his dresser, whispering a savage, "*Shite*," as his toe slammed into the corner of it.

He struggled to unwrap the condom and place it on, before making his way back to bed. Probably swaggering a bit as he did so, but shite it was finally about to happen.

He climbed back onto the bed, pressing a kiss to her belly. "Ready to get up close and personal with Mr. Corn-Fed?"

No reply.

"Lana?"

Silence again, only to be broken by a soft snore.

He rocked back on his heels and sighed. Well fook it all. She'd fallen asleep.

Chapter Eight

"ARE YOU AND Aleck avoiding each other?"

Delonna jumped, spilling half the head on the IPA she was pulling.

"Am I what? Sorry?" She added more beer to the pint and then pushed the handle back up, casting a glance at her friend.

"You heard me." Kenzie's gaze narrowed as she tucked the serving tray beneath her arm. "You guys have said like two words to each other, and even then you barely made eye contact."

Dammit, Kenzie was way too perceptive. Delonna shrugged one shoulder and walked the length of the bar to give the drink to the regular at the end. Only replying to her friend when she returned.

"We're fine. It's just been a busy night."

Kenzie leaned in closer and whispered, "You guys shagged, aye?"

"Kenzie!" *Way* too perceptive. Knowing her ears were turning red, Delonna shook her head. "None of your business."

"I knew it!"

"No. We did not *shag*." Oral sex didn't count as shagging, did it? Officially? Especially when she was so exhausted after a fantastic orgasm that she'd passed out.

A wave of mortification swept through her again and she heaved a sigh. This morning had been awkward to say the least. Waking up in bed alone, with the windstorm having died down to nearly nothing. A glance at her phone had shown they were due at work in just over an hour. She'd found him in the kitchen and had approached with an apology on her lips, but he'd waved it aside and slid a muffin her way. Then he'd disappeared a second later stating he was going to take a cold shower.

She wasn't sure if he'd meant it because the power was still out, or because he'd been blue balled last night. Maybe a little of both.

"Well something happened between the two of you. You've been acting strange around each other all night." Kenzie glanced back toward the pool table room. "Are you going to stay with him again tonight?"

"I assume so." Delonna frowned and shook her head. "Though this is ridiculous. The police haven't found James or any clue of who my attacker was. We both shouldn't be forced out of our house—that we pay rent on, dammit—indefinitely."

"Aye, it's a pain. But better safe than sorry."

"That phrase can suck it. I don't care how applicable it is at the moment."

"Keeps you from running from the inevitable, hmm?" Kenzie gave a knowing laugh and walked away, much too fast for Delonna to hurl a lime wedge at her or something.

She already had one foot in that "inevitable" doorway. And dammit if it hadn't felt pretty fantastic. Maybe it was because she'd been so tired last night, and on edge from the storm, but she'd come harder than ever before with Aleck McLaughlin's head between her legs.

The man was a god at going down.

Her knees went weak and her blood began to pound and she groaned. No, she was absolutely not going to think about that right now.

Drawing in an unsteady breath, she glanced around the pub. It was slowing down, maybe only thirty or so remaining as midnight approached. Kenzie would be off soon, leaving Delonna and Aleck to close.

Despite her protests about having to stay at Aleck's again, she wasn't all that bothered really. It had been kind of nice having someone to go home with. To talk to. To do, ahem, other things with. She could get used to this…

No, you can't. She wasn't looking for a new man, and even her days at the pub were numbered. That last thought sent a pang of disappointment through her, which confused the hell out of her.

Yes, she loved this pub like she owned it herself, but that

was the problem. She didn't. It was Aleck's pride and joy. He would always be the one to hold complete control. To have creative license. To bring in most of the profits.

Which was why she wanted to open one of her own. Well, would open her own once she saved up enough to money to do so. Starting from zero was more than a little disheartening, but not completely impossible.

And she was young. People loved to point it out—well she'd just use the clichéd statement as an encouraging reminder. She had plenty of time to get this dream off the ground.

Leaving the front for a moment, she made her way into the back office. The door was slightly open and she knocked before pushing it fully open.

Aleck glanced up and met her gaze over the laptop. His brows were drawn together in a frown and he didn't seem pleased.

"Bad time? I can come back." She turned, ready to leave, when a female voice stopped her.

"Who's that, Aleck?"

Delonna glanced around, trying to figure out who it had come from. There was no one else in the office.

"It's one of my employees, Ma."

"Delonna?" The voice brightened, her Scottish accent stronger than Aleck's. "I've heard of the lass."

Ah. Aleck had been video chatting with his mom.

"I'll come back when you're done," she said quickly, one

hand on the door.

"Don't leave," his mom argued. "Come around the computer and let me have a look at you."

Slightly alarmed, Delonna raised her gaze to Aleck and mouthed, "What the hell?"

"Ma." Aleck's tone was reproachful. "Delonna must get to work—"

"Nonsense. Send her round. I just want to say hello."

Aleck's lips twisted sardonically and he leaned back in his chair and ran his gaze over her. "There'll be no helping it then. Come around, Delonna."

Oh son of a bitch, really? She had to meet his mom right now? With what had happened last night still running round and round in her head?

Aleck obviously sensed her discomfort because his smile widened. "Unless you're too busy?" he challenged.

Lifting her chin, she made her way around to the other side of the desk. "Not at all."

She came around the desk and found herself face-to-face with Aleck's mom on the monitor. She'd seen the woman at Sarah and Ian's wedding, but hadn't been introduced.

The woman staring back at her resembled Colin and Ian, with their reddish-brown hair. Clearly, Aleck took after his dad.

"Oh, well, aren't you just the prettiest thing. And young." Her gaze shifted to Aleck. "She's quite young for you, don't ya think, Son?"

Delonna glanced sideways and noted he looked a little stricken now.

"She's not so young as to work here, Ma," he said tersely. "Twenty-three, aye, Lana?"

"Twenty-four."

"Hmm." His mom nodded. "That's not exactly what I meant, but I'll let it go. You like working for the pub, lass?"

"I love it here," Delonna admitted honestly. "It's a beautiful pub. Fun, with loyal customers."

"Ah, good then. You realize my husband and I were the first to open and own the place, aye?"

"Yes, I've been told." Delonna glanced at Aleck, and saw his frown deepening.

"All right, you've had your fun, Ma. Let Delonna get back to her work. I don't pay her for idleness, you know."

Not about to let that fly, Delonna whacked him on the shoulder before she thought better of it.

His mother gave a surprised laugh but didn't seem shocked or upset. "Nice to meet you, Delonna."

"You too." She gave a brief smile and turned to leave, but Aleck touched her shoulder.

"Come back in twenty and we'll talk, aye?"

Something in his gaze made her stomach do little flips. "Sure. Sounds good."

With a quick nod, she disappeared, leaving him once again alone.

ALECK COULDN'T HELP but watch her retreating arse, snug in jeans and swinging lightly with each step she took. Memories from last night flitted through his mind and his blood heated a degree.

"I'm still here, ya know, Son."

Shite. Turning his attention back to his mother staring up at him from his computer, he glowered back.

"Aye, you are. And I'll have you know your delay tactic in talking with Delonna isn't appreciated, Ma."

She shrugged innocently. "I remember her a bit from the wedding, but wanted to be properly introduced."

"How is Da?"

Her gaze slid down and she shook her head. "He'll be fine. We weren't going to tell you, because we knew you'd all worry so."

"Aye. Can you blame us?"

Hip surgery. His father had had hip surgery last week, and was slowly recovering. If his mother hadn't slipped and mentioned Da being on painkillers, they might've never known.

"And how are you, Ma?"

"I'm fine. Taking a bit of time off of work to help him with the recovery, but I'm doing all right." The words were said cheerfully enough, but Aleck heard the strain of tension beneath them.

Shite. Why the hell hadn't she mentioned this to them earlier? Da had complained in the past years about his hip aching, but none of his children had realized it had deteriorated to the extent of needing surgery.

"Are you sure he's not up to saying hello?" Aleck asked.

"He's fast asleep from the meds. Unfortunately you just missed him."

"Well give him my love and let him know I'll call him later."

"Will do. All right then, Son, we'll chat soon. I love you."

"Love you too, Ma. Goodbye."

"Cheerio."

He ended their video chat and leaned back in his chair. After a moment he pulled out his phone and sent a group text about Da to his siblings. There would need to be a family meeting, and soon.

After they'd all gotten past the cursing and dismay in the flurry of texts, they agreed to meet for lunch in two days. The general consensus being that one of them would be taking a trip to Edinburgh for a week or so to help their parents and ease their mother from having to take the burden on herself.

Colin, right now, seemed to be the most likely candidate.

There was a swift knock on his office door and Delonna poked her head in again. "Hey, you done?"

"Aye." He set his phone down and leaned back in his chair once more. "Come in."

When she stepped in and closed the door behind her, his

thoughts momentarily slipped from the worry about his da, and to the woman standing in his office.

She didn't say anything for a moment and folded her arms beneath her chest, seeming to hesitate.

"What was it you needed, luv?"

"I um...wanted to know if you remembered to order anymore of the Thistly Cross Whisky Cask Ciders. They seem really popular lately."

He arched a brow. "Aye. Placed an order this afternoon. Was that the only reason you came back here?"

The office was his place of solitude and business. Generally his employees would wait for him to come out or only come in the back if they needed something immediately.

They both knew her question could've waited until he came back out front.

"No. And clearly you know it." She shook her head, her lips twisting wryly. "I want to apologize for last night."

He held back any sign of amusement, and couldn't resist teasing her a bit. "You're going to have to be more specific. Hogging the blankets?"

"Dammit, you know what I mean."

Delonna wasn't really a blusher, but there was a faint hint of pink in her cheeks that fascinated him.

"I fell asleep before we..."

"Ah, yes, that. It's all right."

"Seriously?" She looked both dismayed and irritated. "It's not all right. If the roles had been reversed and you'd gotten yours without me getting mine, I would've woken your ass up."

"You were exhausted," he assured her gently.

Her shoulders slumped and she nodded. "I really was. I hadn't slept well in at least a few days. With the stress of my money disappearing, and then the storm... After that orgasm—which was pretty fucking amazing, by the way—my body just gave out on me and crashed. Without my permission."

To hear her describe her orgasm as "pretty fucking amazing" had his cock waking up and his blood pounding harder. Because now all he could envision was her flat on her back with her legs over his shoulders again and his tongue inside her.

He struggled to keep his cock from reaching full hard-on status and drew in a slow breath. "I can wait for you, Lana."

She reached behind her and locked the door. "I know. And you're pretty sweet about it, but I'd like to make it up to you."

When she strode toward his desk there was no willing his cock back down. His heart quickened, both in alarm and anticipation.

"Make it up to me? Now?"

"Oh *aye*, boss boy." She gave a husky laugh and came around his desk. Pushing his wheeled chair back a few inches, she went to her knees in front of him.

Chapter Nine

"LANA," ALECK RASPED, half protesting as she reached for his zipper.

When she pulled him free and into her hands, he couldn't have stopped her if the pub were on fire.

"Jesus, I think I'm going to start calling you boss *man*." Her words were low and uneven.

And with that, she took him in her mouth, and all ability to think was gone. Thank God she'd had the sense to lock the door.

Her mouth was hot and wet, her pink tongue quick and talented as it teased him. Shite, but every little move was incredible.

He reached down to grab her ponytail, twisting the soft slippery strands around his hand as she gave him probably the bloody best blow job of his life. Fast and then slow, taking him shallow and then deep. She explored every inch of him, creating a pleasure that was so completely intense. Bringing him right to the edge of ecstasy.

All too soon, he knew he was going to come, and he

struggled to remember how to talk. He pushed at her weakly, to warn her, but she refused to move. With her hands on his thighs, she instead took him deeper. Then it was too late. Minutes later she was rocking back on her heels and licking her lips.

"Lana," he muttered thickly, still in a complete daze. "That was...pretty fucking amazing, as you put it."

"Good." Her eyes shined with pleasure and maybe a hint of self-consciousness. "I think that makes up for last night."

He caught her arm as she tried to move away, pulling her forward.

"Tonight my cock won't be in your mouth, but inside your delicious body, luv." He touched her lips with his thumb, before pressing a hard kiss on them. "But only after I taste you again and have you screaming my name."

"You are a dirty man," she whispered, but her eyes shone with excitement.

"Aye. I think we're equal in that regard."

"I think you may be right." Her gaze turned contemplative. "Now, I'd better get back up front before people start talking."

He waited until she'd reached the door before calling out, "You know, they're already talking."

"I do." She paused and then gave him a lopsided grin. "And I really couldn't give two shits anymore. You're worth the risk."

After she'd gone, he pondered her words. *You're worth*

the risk.

They sent a little thrill of pleasure through his spent body, but in the logical side of his brain, the alarm bells started to go off.

This was the first time he'd ever gotten involved with an employee, and "risk" was putting it mildly. But there was no turning back now, and he really didn't have the faintest desire to do so anyway.

He just hoped it wouldn't come back to bite him in the arse.

~

"DID KENZIE ALREADY leave?"

Delonna nodded at Aleck's question, not glancing up from her tip money she counted. A moment later she wrapped a rubber band around it and slipped it into her purse.

"About ten minutes ago. She said to send her love." She lifted her head to look at Aleck.

He leaned against the bar, arms folded across his broad chest, and a lazy gaze sliding over her. Lazy, predatory gaze.

A shiver of excitement raced down her spine as she thought about his promise from earlier tonight. A promise to basically screw her silly. He'd spoken those enflaming words right after she'd… The image floated through her head of just exactly what she'd done to him.

Had she ever been so brazen? So completely uncaring of

her surroundings? So eager to just drop to her knees and give someone a blow job in the middle of a work shift? Never until Aleck. She'd lost her ever-loving mind. Yet she couldn't bring herself to regret it.

He must've seen the look in her eyes because he unfurled himself from where he lounged at the bar and approached her.

Her quickening pulse jumped even faster and subconsciously she took a step backward. His soft laugh only raised the fine hairs on her arms and sent tingles of anticipation through her.

"Shouldn't we head back to your place?" she asked, her voice uneven.

"We will in a bit." He stopped right in front of her and reached out to tug the elastic band from her hair, sending the blonde strands sliding down her back. "I've been waiting quite impatiently, all evening, to have another moment alone with you."

She couldn't help a breathy laugh. "Did I leave you unsatisfied earlier?"

"Unsatisfied? Silly lass, you left me a melted puddle. I couldn't move for at least a half hour." He smiled, running his thumb and forefinger over a strand of hair. "But you did all the giving and I had no opportunity to touch in return."

Her pulse jumped wildly. "Well, that is a damn shame, isn't it?"

"Aye." He moved his hands to her waist, stroking his

thumbs over the sides of her stomach. "And I've been thinking about your mouth ever since."

She inhaled unevenly and lifted a brow. "My mouth?"

"Mmm." He lowered his head, so their breath mingled. "You have these lush, full pink lips that I love to kiss."

He brushed his mouth over hers, so lightly that goose bumps rose on her body. She reached to hold his shoulders, not sure she could stand all too well anymore.

"That I love to nibble upon." He caught her bottom lip between his teeth and tugged lightly.

All too soon he released it and stroked his tongue over the flesh, the gesture both soothing and arousing. Her fingers curled around his muscled shoulders, her nails scraping at him over his shirt.

He lifted his head slightly. "You have no idea how much I want to be inside you right now, Lana."

There was no chance to breathe before his mouth crashed down on hers, not gentle or teasing, but in a possessive, heated claiming.

She opened to him, meeting his tongue with her own as her blood turned to fire from his aggression and words.

The hands that were at her waist slid to cup her bottom, lifting her easily off the ground so she could wrap her legs around him.

He held her, his tongue making love to her mouth as he carried her over to the pool table. He sat her on the edge, his hips thrusting between hers, making her feel his hardened flesh even through their layers of denim.

The heat between her legs bloomed into a frenzy of fire. She moaned, pressing herself against his thrusts. She wanted him inside her. Now. She couldn't walk outside into that cold air, drive home and then start over. No. Her body was awake and desperate for his touch. Ready to explode like a firework with a lit fuse.

She pulled her mouth from his and whispered a ragged, "Please, Aleck."

He broke the kiss and without a word, caught her shirt in his hands to tug it up and off her body. He discarded her black bra a moment later.

"Shite," he hissed, cupping the fullness of her breasts in his hands. "These have been giving me hard-ons for too damn long now. So lush." He leaned down and kissed one nipple and it puckered against his lips. "Beautiful. I couldn't see them last night in the darkness."

When he drew the tip into his mouth, she cried out and arched her back. He suckled the tip, lightly and then hard. She thrust her fingers into his hair, silently showing him she didn't want him to be gentle. And then not so silently with her low groan of pleasure when he lightly bit the swollen tip.

He made a low, very-much-male growl and transferred his mouth to the other breast. He'd caught on fast to what she liked, because his mouth was firm and merciless. Sucking and biting, bringing her arousal to fever pitch.

She let out a cry of protest when he lifted his head, but it ended on a gasp as he lifted her from the table and set her on her feet. No words were spoken as he deftly turned her around so her back was to him.

He nuzzled the back of her neck, pressing a kiss against her nape. He slid his arm around her waist and his hand moved to splay over her belly. It rubbed the flesh there and she had a moment of self-consciousness, because it wasn't a flat stomach by any means. But the insecurity disappeared just as quickly and she relaxed against him, loving the way his breath quickened. Grew deeper.

She rocked her bottom back against his erection and he groaned, his arm tightening around her waist as he thrust against her.

With skilled fingers he unfastened her jeans, tugging them and her panties over her hips and down her legs. She kicked off her shoes and stepped out of the clothes.

While he was fully clothed, she was completely naked. It should've made her feel vulnerable. Exposed. But instead it empowered her. With a purr of pleasure she rubbed back against him again.

There was no worry about waiting until they got home anymore. Clearly if he'd stripped her, he intended to have sex here. Maybe even on the pool table. Through her dazed thoughts, she realized that would be a first.

His arm returned around her waist, and he smoothed his hand over her stomach and then downward, to cup the flesh between her legs.

She rose to her tiptoes and rocked back against him. "Aleck..."

"Mmm. Yes, luv."

He curled a finger into her aching channel and she shuddered with pleasure.

"Oh God, just don't stop."

"Wasn't even considering it." He added a second finger, sliding them both deep, before bringing one up to touch her clit.

Her body reacted like she'd received an electric shock, jerking and making her mind go white for a moment. He held the reins to her pleasure and wasn't letting go.

Dimly, while he teased that sensitive spot, she was aware of his other hand caressing her bottom. He squeezed the flesh there, while rolling and pinching her clit.

Her breaths were ragged now, her moans low. She knew how close she was to the edge. The sharp whack and the slight sting of pain brought her back from the cliff of pleasure momentarily. But it rushed right back when she realized he'd smacked her ass.

Shock warred with pleasure and she lifted her head, trying to turn and look at him, but the second smack had her gasping and turning her gaze straight ahead again.

"That's for making me be quite unprofessional earlier, luv." His palm connected with her bottom again and she moaned. "Really quite naughty of you to go into your boss' office and give him a blow job."

"I didn't hear you complain—oh!" Her breathy reply ended on another gasp of shock and pleasure as his smack connected harder.

"I think you hinted to me once about liking to be spanked," he murmured against her ear. "It looks as if that wasn't just a frivolous remark."

No, it hadn't been. But she couldn't remember having said that to him before. She must've though, because he was here, bending her over the pool table and smacking her bottom. And she was loving every moment of it.

The spanking continued. Light and then harder, all while he continued to play with her clit. The need and heat inside her grew higher and faster. She moved against his hand, both arching into his hand between her legs and the hand that would lash across her ass.

"You look amazing," he muttered thickly, his lips moving over her nape. "With my red handprint staining your pretty white arse."

"*Aleck.*"

He caught her earlobe between his teeth and tugged lightly, his finger moving faster between her legs now.

"*Ohmygod.*" She gasped, throwing her head back against his shoulder as she ground against his hand. "So close."

He smacked her bottom again, hard, and sank a finger deep into her sex. The combination sent her flying and screaming his name as she climaxed.

Her world was out of control, her mind a complete void

as ecstasy took hold. Her legs gave out a moment later, and he caught her before she could hit the floor.

ALECK TURNED HER gently in his arms, holding her boneless weight up as he pressed a soft kiss to her lips.

He hadn't been attempting dirty talk by remarking on the beauty of her arse. It truly was amazing. Almost as amazing as the fact that she'd loved getting spanked, because he certainly enjoyed carrying out the act.

Picking her up, he laid her on the pool table. He slid his hands beneath her thighs to pull her forward, so her arse was on the wooden lip of the table. He smoothed his palms down her thighs, staring down at her lush, pale body laid out like a damn present for him. He'd take her here, just like this.

"Wow," she murmured, her gaze still drugged with passion, "I did not see that coming."

"The swats?"

Her mouth curled into a lazy smile. "Yeah. You've got a naughty side."

His laugh was tight with the driving need to just take her. "Aye. And it seems you love it."

"Hell yeah I do. You can spank my ass any day, boss boy."

She stretched her arms above her head to grab the other side of the pool table. The move lifted her breasts, showing a small mole beneath one.

Unable to resist, he leaned down to kiss it, while cupping the softness of the breast in his palm.

She made a murmur of pleasure and her hips lifted in the silent signal that she needed more. Wanted him.

He straightened and dug into his pocket for the condom he'd grabbed. After undoing his fly and unzipping his jeans, he shoved them and his briefs below his knees.

Relief and anticipation flickered in her eyes. "I thought you were going to make us wait until we got back to your place."

"That may have been the plan at one point, but the more time went by, the more I wanted you." He pulled his cock free and placed the condom on it. "I came out of my office ready to fook you silly, lass."

He heard her breath catch, whether at his words, or from the sight of him so completely hard and ready.

Her lashes fluttered down and she lifted her hips slightly. "Then what are you waiting for? Clearly I'm ready and willing. Pretty damn willing, actually."

Choking on a laugh, and needing no more encouragement, he slid his hands to cup her arse and pull her forward so he was positioned perfectly between her legs.

He reached down to grasp himself, rubbing his cock back and forth over the glistening pink folds of her sex before slowly sliding it in.

The hot, warm suck of her flesh drew him deeper, and

the air hissed out from between his clenched teeth.

When he lifted his gaze from where he entered her, to her face, he saw her lips parted on a silent moan and her eyes closed; dark lashes fanning out over flushed cheeks. Need swelled in him and he thrust deep, filling her completely and wrenching a soft gasp from Delonna.

He stayed buried inside her, taking a moment to revel in the feel of her for a moment.

"Have I hurt you?" he managed to ask, unevenly.

"No." Her head moved from side to side, and she drew in a ragged breath. "You feel perfect. Incredible."

"And I'll say the same for you." He began to move slowly inside her and was rewarded by her soft sigh. "You don't know how long I've wanted this, Lana. How long I've wanted you."

Her lashes fluttered up and she met his gaze as he eased deeper again into her. "Knowing I couldn't have you because you were with that arsehole."

Surprise flickered in her eyes, but still she stayed silent.

"When you would walk by, flirting so outrageously with me, something inside me went completely caveman. I imagined this." He slid his gaze from the top of her head down to where they were joined.

"Here?" she whispered, a tiny line formed between her brows.

"Aye. I imagined grabbing you, stripping you and taking you on this bloody pool table." He pulled slowly out. "*Just.*" Thrust hard. "*Like.*" Sank deep. "*This.*"

She cried out and there was no lightness or teasing in her expression anymore, just a sparkle of realization and acceptance in her pleasure-drugged eyes.

"*Aleck.*"

He didn't mind it when she called him boss boy; it was a fun little teasing thing between them. But he loved it when she said his name, especially when it was on a needy whimper of desire.

He moved harder, completely losing all ability to hold a conversation, as pure need drove him. He tightened his hold on her arse, lifting her to make their joining even snugger. He knew he'd leave bruises on the insides of her thighs. They'd probably go well with the marks he was no doubt leaving on her arse from gripping it so hard.

His body tightened as release approached. He moved his hand to touch Delonna, but she was already climaxing. Her back arched and she cried out—the hot grip of her body tightening further around him.

With a strangled yell he buried himself deep and allowed the release to take him in waves of pleasure. Until his legs were shaking and his mind was empty. He dragged in ragged gasps of air, staring down at her, limp on the table. Her body spent and flushed with pleasure. Her eyes once more closed.

"God, Lana, you were worth the bloody wait."

With his legs threatening to give out, he fell forward on top of her.

Just in time to miss the glass shards from the window that exploded as the pub was riddled with bullets.

Chapter Ten

"...SIGNIFICANT DAMAGE... YOUR insurance will cover it."

Aleck nodded, absorbing Colin's words even as he kept one eye on the deputy interviewing Delonna.

They'd been lucky as hell. If it had happened thirty seconds sooner he might've been hit by gunfire, or at the very least hit by the shattering glass.

Someone had shot up his pub. Had deliberately fired several rounds of a semi-automatic into the front window of his pub. The flimsy drapes had been pulled shut at closing—so no one would've seen what kind of trouble he and Delonna were up to.

But Aleck wasn't the slightest bit convinced the incident was random. He couldn't believe it was a couple of teenagers or drunks out having fun. He suspected the person who'd shot up the pub was the same man who'd gone after Delonna earlier in the week.

As if sensing his gaze on her, she glanced up and met his stare. A look of torment flashed in her eyes, before she looked away and resumed answering the deputy's questions.

Aleck had finished being questioned not moments earlier.

"She all right?"

Aleck glanced at his brother who'd spoken.

"Delonna? Aye, I think so. She was a bit more shaken up than I was, though, when it happened."

"Mmm. I can imagine. Quite late for you both to still have been here, aye?"

There was no denying the speculation in Colin's tone, or the knowing look in his eyes.

"We were talking." And by talking he meant shagging.

"Ah, right. Of course you were." Amusement danced momentarily in Colin's otherwise grim gaze.

Shite, they'd gotten dressed in record time after Aleck had placed a call to the police. Delonna had been in the midst of disinfecting the pool table when the police had arrived.

Colin had of course been texted and informed, in what must have been some sort of silent code in the law enforcement community. When it came to family, you got notified immediately.

"I don't like the looks of this," Colin admitted. "I think whoever did this is after Delonna and is likely the same bloke who attacked her at her home."

Aleck gave a short nod. "Agreed. Have they learned anything about the first attack? Any suspects?"

"Unfortunately, no. And no leads on locating the ex-boyfriend either."

Aleck swore softly. "All this violence and these threats have fallen on her, and she'd nothing to do with her ex's quandaries."

"Aye, the poor lass." Colin gave him a considering look. "You seem quite a bit concerned with Delonna, and a bit less so about your pub."

"Don't be daft." Aleck glowered at his brother. "I'm bloody livid that my pub was on the receiving end of this bastart."

They both glanced over at someone who was collecting the shell casings. More officers were outside checking to see if any evidence was left behind.

"But I'm worried for Delonna," Colin admitted, lowering his voice. "Whoever this bloke is, his 'warnings' are just escalating in danger. You're lucky neither of you was injured, or even killed, tonight."

"I know." His jaw clenched as he struggled to control his anger and fear for Delonna's safety.

"She'll remain at your house?"

"Aye, of course." He shook his head. "I'm not sure it's enough anymore, though."

"What are you thinking?"

Aleck pulled his gaze away from the bar counter. He was thinking that bloody deputy was going to dismantle the counter trying to get a bullet out of it.

"I'm not quite certain," he muttered, "but I'll let you know when I am."

With that, he strode off to tell the deputy to go easy on his pub.

ᔕ

"WHERE ARE YOU off to?"

Delonna flinched and halted in her attempts to quickly escape to the spare bedroom.

"I was going to head to bed. I'm not really up for watching a movie tonight," she murmured, trying not to meet his gaze.

"Aye, I'm quite tired too and sleeping sounds amazing after the night we've had. But you're going the wrong way, luv. My room's at the other end of the hall."

Now she did lift her gaze, unable to hide the skepticism in it. "You want me to sleep in your room?"

"Aye. You did last night, and I quite like the idea of having you in my bed again." He paused, appearing a little chagrined as a sexy smile crossed his face. "Just a bit of cuddling, of course. I think we're both too tired for much more."

He was right on that last part.

"Last night I pretty much forced myself into your room because of the storm. You don't need to feel obligated—"

"It's no obligation, Lana." He moved slowly toward her, until they were just inches apart, and he reached down to take her hand. "It's me enjoying the feel of having you in my arms. Knowing you're safe."

His voice cracked just the tiniest bit on that last word, and her heart quickened. He cared about her. He wasn't saying it, but she could see it in his eyes and in the not-quite-hidden emotion in his voice.

"All right." Before she could second-guess herself, she nodded.

Only some minutes later, when they were buried under the covers with their bodies spooned together, did she start to wonder if this had been smart.

A needy part inside her had jumped at his unspoken offer of support—just the opportunity to be held. How long had it been since she'd had that? Not with James. If she let herself admit it, he hadn't really been more than good sex, and the occasional concert and dinner out.

Aleck was different. Everything about the way she was with him was different. And what she'd thought was good sex with James had turned out to be just decent. Sex was amazing with Aleck.

With her body tucked up against his, a protective muscled arm around her waist and her head tucked beneath his chin, she couldn't deny the possibility that she was falling for him a little.

No man had ever made her feel this safe and protected before. Feel so at peace, even when her world was chaos. And for this moment, she'd take that mental escape from all the bad crap going on.

A pang of guilt hit that her troubles had now spilled over

into Aleck's world.

"I'm sorry," she said softly.

"You're supposed to be asleep."

"I know. I'm halfway there." And she was. Being held like this relaxed her to the point that sleep just meant closing her eyes for a few minutes and trying to turn off her mind.

"You can stop apologizing. You did so both in the pub and the drive home. This isn't your fault, and you can stop blaming yourself."

"Maybe not intentionally my fault, but I dated the asshole who turned out to have some really awful acquaintances."

"Again, not your fault. It could've happened to anyone, Lana." He kissed the top of her head. "Forget about it for now and get some sleep."

She closed her eyes, trying to stop the barrage of thoughts in her mind. It worked for the most part, but one scene from the night began to flicker through her memory. Sex on the pool table. The whole thing had been so sensual and so naughty. And she'd loved every minute of it. Something he'd said during had stuck in her head.

And now, she couldn't help saying softly, "My flirting wasn't completely harmless by the way."

"Hmm?" His reply was a drowsy murmur.

"When we were in the middle of sex, you brought up my flirting. I meant it to come off as flippant and harmless when I would flirt with you in the last few years." She hesitated.

"But there was a part of me that meant it. A part of me that was so completely drawn to you, even though I was with someone else."

The arm around her waist tightened, and she wished they were face-to-face so she could see his expression.

"Well," he finally murmured, "clearly I should've seduced you earlier."

A tired laugh escaped her. "Clearly. Though if you remember, I started this all."

"Mmm, and I'll finish it."

Before she'd realized his intent, he'd shifted and eased her onto her back. Her breath caught as he braced himself on one elbow beside her and kissed her belly.

"Again?" Her eyes widened. "I thought you were tired."

"Apparently I'm never too tired for you."

He kissed lower and lower, until she was still and waiting for his mouth to reach its target destination.

Her pulse was going a mile a minute as she parted her thighs for him. He immediately repositioned his body so he was lying between her legs, and a moment later his mouth found what it sought.

The touch of his tongue on her most sensitive spot had her hips rising and her reaching blindly to grip his hair. Unlike the hard frenzied sex from earlier, this was gentle yet equally sensual.

After just minutes of his steady exploration of her body with his tongue, she was falling apart with a soft cry of pleasure. A moment later he had on a condom and eased inside her. His strokes just as gentle and unhurried as his mouth has been.

It was that stage of being equally exhausted and aroused, and she felt almost meditative in the way her body accepted the thick length of him. They found a languid rhythm, and she knew he was just as close to release as she was. When they both reached their peaks it was nearly simultaneously.

Afterward her heartbeat returned to normal and they were a tangle of limbs beneath the covers. She pressed a kiss to his shoulder, loving the weight of his body—so potently hard and male—on hers.

"Sleep now?" she murmured.

"Sleep now," he agreed, and moved off her. He took a second to toss the condom into the garbage, before he returned and they were once again cuddling.

Delonna frowned slightly. Already there was an ease between them that was more akin to a couple who'd been together for years. Not two people who'd only just become lovers.

As her mind drifted off to sleep, she again had to accept the knowledge that she'd let him inside her heart, and much too fast. She needed to figure out a way to stop it. But it was hard to hit the brakes on a runaway train.

"I HOPE YOU haven't any plans, because we're having dinner

at Sarah and Ian's place."

At the *excuse me* look on Delonna's face, Aleck realized he might've phrased that a bit better.

"I mean, if you'd like to join us, we'd appreciate your presence," he corrected, with a lazy grin.

"From an inarguable command, to an all-kinds-of-proper invite," she drawled.

She paused in the midst of folding laundry—which was still a bit odd to him, having a female besides his ma sorting through his underwear, but she'd insisted on being useful if she stayed here.

He'd arranged their schedules to be aligned so he could both keep her safe, if need be, and they could carpool together. At least that's what he'd told her. He quite fancied sharing his free time with her.

It was certainly convenient when he had the itch to stop everything and drag her off to the bedroom to shag. Or the couch. Or even in the kitchen. They'd broken in all those places since he'd brought her here to stay.

"Aren't these dinners a family thing?" she asked, arching a brow as she folded a pair of his jeans.

"Aye, but you've become a significant presence in our little group." And now that they were sleeping together, maybe even a bit more.

She shook her head, and her ponytail swung adorably. Shite, everything was adorable about her right now. The pink plaid flannel pajama bottoms, and the tight gray top that hugged her lovely breasts.

"Aleck..." She sighed. "I don't want you to feel like you have to stay with me twenty-four seven. That you feel obligated to bring me to family events."

He closed the distance between them, catching her wrist and tugging her to him. She dropped the jeans in her grasp and slid into his arms.

"I want you to come tonight." He pressed a soft kiss to her equally soft lips. "Everyone there already loves you and will be more put out if you're not there."

She grimaced. "You're not just saying this—"

"I swear I'm not." He kissed her longer this time. "I want you near me." A deeper kiss now, and she seemed to melt into him. "To make sure you're protected."

She seemed to stiffen at that last comment and pulled away slightly.

"To keep me protected," she said softly. "Of course."

Something about the way she said it made him frown slightly.

"What time is dinner?" she asked, turning back to the laundry.

"Five thirty."

"Well then I'd better get the day started. I want to go running before then."

"I'll come."

"No." She shook her head and averted her gaze. "Really, it's my alone time. Almost meditative and gives me moments to gather my thoughts."

He wouldn't force it, but he did hate the idea of her out there alone with all that had happened. "You know," he said quickly, "I have a fantastic treadmill in the garage that would—"

"Thanks, but I'm an outside runner." She grabbed the laundry basket and moved past him. "I'll be done and ready by four though."

He watched her leave, adorable rounded ass swishing, and bit back a groan. Too bad he couldn't talk her into another, more sensual form of exercise.

"HOW ARE THE steaks coming?"

Aleck stepped into the kitchen where his brothers were taking their once-a-month turn at preparing dinner.

"Brilliantly. They should be done shortly," Colin replied, as he leaned back against the counter.

Ian grinned. "Aye, trust you to show up when all the work has already been done."

"I'm here now." Aleck tossed a bag of lettuce on the table. "And I've brought the requested salad."

Colin's brows drew together. "You've brought a bag of leaves."

"That counts as a salad. I'm not wrong."

Ian snorted and shook his head. "Such a pretty face, and yet the man can't even make a proper salad. Fortunately

Sarah has trained me well."

Ian made his way to the fridge and pulled out several bottles of dressing, and several other toppings.

"Did you convince Delonna to come tonight?" Colin asked, as he ripped open the bag of lettuce and dumped it in a bowl.

"Aye. She's out playing with Ian's children. I gave her no choice on coming, really. I wasn't about to leave her alone."

"And you shouldn't." Ian rinsed a container of cherry tomatoes in the sink and dumped them on top of the lettuce. "The whole situation has slipped from dodgy to downright dangerous."

"It has," Aleck agreed. "It's not safe for her here. I'm not even sure *I* can keep her protected."

"You've a gun though, right?" Ian asked, sprinkling some feta cheese onto the salad now.

"Aye," he admitted grimly. "And I'll use it if need be." And right now, it was looking more likely.

"I could speak with some folks at the department and arrange a safe place for her, Aleck," Colin said. "This is getting a bit intense."

"No." He didn't care for the idea of anyone else watching over Delonna. Not a bit. "She's under my protection."

"Quite gallant of you really. And for someone who's just an employee of yours, aye?" Ian's lips twisted. "Maybe a friend too."

Knowing where this was going, Aleck kept his own

mouth closed and refused to take the bait.

"Friend with benefits," Colin murmured.

Ian gave a short guffaw and returned to the salad with a bag of candied pecans.

"If you're trying to wind me up, it's not working," Aleck drawled.

"Is it not?" Ian asked.

Well, maybe it was. Realizing he was clenching his fists at his sides, Aleck relaxed his grip.

"Before you arrived," Ian continued, "we were making wagers on how long you and Delonna lasted—when she came to stay with you—before you started shagging."

"That is none of your fookin' business," Aleck roared as he lost his attempt to appear unfazed. "Ah, you bloody wankers."

His brothers laughed, as Aleck strode to the fridge to grab a beer.

"He's not so good taking it as he is in dishing it out," Colin murmured to his twin.

"No, can't say that he is." Ian grinned. "You're right, we're just winding you up. We quite like Delonna, and are happy to see you dating—"

"We're not dating." He popped off the cap on the beer and took a swig.

They were sleeping together. Two very different things. There were no romantic dinners out. No strolls on the beach holding hands. It was sex with a friend. So, aye, Colin was right in a way. Friends with benefits. Still, he wasn't about to confirm it aloud.

The silence from his brothers had him glancing up from his own brooding thoughts and meeting the twins' equally matched contemplative stares.

Aleck took another sip. "What?"

"It's not such a bad thing to seek out a relationship," Colin said cautiously.

"For another man, no, likely not. For someone like me? Aye, it would be." His fingers clenched around the bottle. "I'm not interested in that sort of thing."

"You truly don't want a wife someday? Children?" Ian asked, visibly confounded.

There was the familiar, invisible punch in the stomach if he let his mind go there. For a moment he was sixteen again, running through the wynds of Edinburgh, stealing kisses with a gorgeous brunette. Just as quickly as they came, he reeled the memories back in. Eased that wall back up around his heart.

"It's not my cup of tea."

"I thought it might just be a phase." Colin went to check on the steaks. "Seeing you with Delonna gave us all a bit of hope. You're different with her."

"Aye, well it's hard to send her home afterward, when she's staying with me," Aleck said tersely.

Only a handful of seconds went by before the woman they were discussing strode into the room.

"Hey guys," Delonna said, turning her bright smile on all three of them. "Mind if I grab a beer?"

"Not at all. Help yourself." Ian gestured to the fridge.

"Thanks."

If Delonna had overheard any of the conversation about her, she didn't give any indication.

"Smells amazing in here. Thanks for letting me come tonight." She easily removed the beer cap and took a drink.

Shite, but his mind was in the gutter. Just that sentence and the way her lips wrapped around the bottle head had Aleck's blood heating. He wouldn't mind helping her come later as well.

Her gaze met his for a moment, and there was a twinkle of mischief in her eyes, before she finished her long pull on the beer.

"You're always welcome here, Delonna," Ian said with a warm smile. "And I hope you never doubt that."

Her attention shifted to Ian and her tone quieted. "I really appreciate that. Appreciate everything you've all done."

"How could we not? You're like family," Colin added. "We care about you."

Aleck was aware of Colin turning a pointed look at him, but he chose to ignore it. He kept his attention completely on Delonna. It was hard to see her as he once did. A cute, flirty bartender who worked for him. After last night every part of him reacted to her on a primal, possessive level.

He wanted to pick her up and carry her off and away

from his family. Then strip her out of that sweater dress and boots and shag her silly.

While his brothers might have romantic ideals about him and Delonna, he wasn't so naïve. Lust came easily. Love was much harder. And right now he was completely over his head in lust with Delonna. Likely would be until they'd shagged for a few weeks and took the edge off.

As if sensing his thoughts, she glanced his way again. Her eyes widened and he watched her breasts rise slightly as she drew in a quick breath.

She touched her neck, almost self-consciously, and lowered her gaze.

"Anyway, I should get back to the ladies." She turned to hurry from the room, calling out, "Which, by the way, Ian, you and Sarah make adorable children."

"Thank you," Ian murmured as she left, then turned to Aleck. "She's a special girl. I certainly hope we can keep her from being hurt."

Aleck grunted. "I've already told you I'm going to do everything I can to ensure her safety."

"I don't doubt it." Ian grabbed the salad and headed toward the dining room, saying grimly as he passed, "But I actually meant being hurt by you."

Chapter Eleven

"I LOVE MY nephew, but he's breaking my arm." Kenzie groaned and adjusted the sleeping newborn. "Anyone else want to hold him for a bit?"

Delonna hesitated from where she sat on the couch, glancing at the sleeping baby. He'd made the rounds to all the other women in the room except her. Her fingers curled and the urge to volunteer was tempered with the unease of not really being experienced with newborns.

She waited to see if Hailey would volunteer, since Sarah was outside with her daughter Emily at the moment. But Hailey seemed busy pilfering the bowl of nuts, clearly looking for one type in particular.

"Delonna? You've not held Ben yet." Kenzie stood, and without waiting for her to accept, gently laid the sleeping baby in her arms. "There you are."

Delonna caught her breath, almost afraid to breathe, fearing it would wake him. He was so tiny and beautiful with his dark hair and hint of olive-toned skin—those traits from his mom. She knew, when his eyes were opened, that they were the striking green all the McLaughlins had.

"He's precious, aye?" Kenzie murmured, smiling down at them.

"He is," she said softly, drawing her finger down one super-soft cheek. The baby's mouth puckered, but he stayed asleep.

"He'll be hungry soon, I imagine." Kenzie laughed. "We'll hand him back to his ma after that, as you won't be able to help with that so much."

That had a smile tugging at Delonna's lips.

Hailey made a noise of triumph as she found the nut she was seeking and popped it in her mouth.

"I'm going to grab a soda and see if the men need anything," she said a moment later. "Need anything from the kitchen?"

Kenzie and Delonna shook their heads and murmured a no thanks.

"I'm sorry Brett couldn't make it tonight." Delonna glanced at her friend.

"Ah, me too, but he's come down with a disgusting cold and I told him he'd best stay home and not risk giving it to the baby."

"Good call. Will you bring him a plate of leftovers?"

"Of course. And a bit of whisky." Kenzie's smile seemed a little mischievous after the whisky remark. But before Delonna could comment on it, Kenzie asked, "So you must be quite shaken up about what happened at the pub."

Delonna's stomach knotted. "I am, and I feel really guilty about it."

"You needn't feel guilt. It's not as if you were the one who pulled the trigger." Kenzie shook her head as she sat down on the couch next to her. "I'm shocked it's gotten this violent, so quickly."

"Me too." She stared down at Ben, registering the complete vulnerability and innocence of the baby in her arms. Maybe she shouldn't even be holding him right now. Everything she touched seemed to become a target.

"How are you and Aleck getting on?"

Choose your words carefully. "Just fine. He's been very supportive and nice to me."

"A bit more than nice, hmm?" Kenzie drawled. "No use pretending you're not shagging now. You've a terrible poker face."

Delonna smiled, knowing her friend was right. "I know I do."

"Well, it's good you're having fun together. He'll be a nice distraction from the chaos around you. And from that arse of an ex of yours."

A distraction. She hadn't even thought of Aleck that way, had she? It had just been instinctive and seemingly inevitable that they'd end up in bed together.

"It makes me happy to see him with you too. You're different than the usual women he gets involved with," Kenzie went on. "Not all trashy or dimwitted."

"Um, thank you?" was all she managed, not quite sure how to reply to that. She really didn't want to imagine Aleck in bed with other women, especially some that had likely come into the bar. Just picturing him going to bed with some of those bimbos made her feel a little stabby.

"Aye, it's a compliment," Kenzie assured her and then hesitated.

"There's a but?"

"Mmm." Kenzie gave a small smile. "Just as I said before, be careful with him and make sure you're keeping your heart out of things."

Frowning slightly, Delonna avoided her friend's gaze. Yes, Aleck had a reputation as being a commitment-phobe, but Kenzie hadn't seen how he'd been lately with her. Delonna knew she wasn't imagining the tenderness in him when he was with her. The way he held her all night long, and would press a kiss to her forehead when he thought she slept.

"It might be nothing, but there was someone else. A long time ago." Kenzie interrupted her thoughts.

"Sorry?"

"Aleck. He had a girlfriend in Scotland, and though he kept the relationship fairly quiet, I knew they were very close."

Before Kenzie could finish, or Delonna could ask what happened to the relationship, the kitchen door swung open and the men filed into the living room.

"Dinner's about ready," Ian announced. "I hope you're all hungry…and can anybody tell me where my wife went?"

"Outside with Emily." Kenzie gestured to the window. "And about time, I'm bloody well starving."

Everyone went different ways, most to the kitchen, and Delonna was left with a snoozing newborn in her arms. Her thoughts still lingered with mild curiosity on this former girlfriend Aleck had back in Scotland.

"You look quite motherly right now."

She glanced up, not realizing Aleck was still in the room.

"Do I?" An amused smile twisted her lips. "Well, it's much easier borrowing someone else's baby for a few minutes than having one of your own."

"Doubtless." He stared down at her, his expression somehow both wary and tender. "Mind if I take a turn and hold my nephew?"

"Please do." Before she could stand up and hand Ben off, Aleck reached down to lift him out of her arms.

There was something intimate about the trade-off, and her breath caught as their gazes locked. And then Ben was in his arms and Aleck's attention turned fully to the baby.

She watched Aleck cradle the infant, touching his cheek as he silently stared down at his nephew. A myriad of expressions crossed Aleck's face. Wonder. Tenderness. But it was the brief flicker of sadness that made a bunch of questions zip through Delonna's mind.

Did he want kids of his own? Maybe he was feeling the

strain of being the oldest McLaughlin sibling and not being married or having any children. Maybe he couldn't even have children.

Her phone buzzed with a text message, and she dug into her pocket to get it. She didn't recognize the number, but after reading the message her easygoing mood vanished and her stomach went sour.

"Who is it?" Aleck didn't miss a thing. "You've lost all the color in your face."

"It's..." She shook her head, swallowing hard. "It's James. He wrote me."

"Give me the phone." Without waiting for her to do so, Aleck cradled the baby in one arm and plucked the phone free from her grasp with the other.

He read aloud the text, "'Heard about the pub and other shit. Sorry, babe. I was in trouble, needed money and had to disappear. Guess you got pulled into my mess. I didn't think he'd remember you. This guy doesn't play around. Be careful. Maybe disappear if you can. Anyway, it's been fun. Stay...'" Aleck didn't finish, his lips tightening into an angry slash.

She knew what it said. How he'd ended the text. *Stay fuckable.* Again, she had to wonder how the *good sex* blinders had managed to block out what a complete asshole he was. Again she reflected on how what she'd thought was good sex was *nothing* compared to what she and Aleck had.

"I swear I'll kill him myself if I find the bastart," he said savagely. "Colin needs to see this, or whoever is working on your case at the station."

She nodded, not about to argue. "Unfortunately, it's not his number."

"But it's *a* number and it has to lead to someone."

Before he could continue his argument, there was a flurry of movement and a squealed, "Uncle Aleck!"

Emily bounded into the room and threw her arms around his waist.

"Ah, my little Em." He visibly relaxed, an effort Delonna knew was forced rather than natural. He was still livid.

"Though not such a little lass anymore, aye?" He gave her a smile. "My God, you're almost a teenager now."

"Totally." She stood up on her tiptoes to kiss her newborn brother on the cheek. "And isn't Ben just the cutest? Mom says I need to take all the proper classes before I babysit."

"A decent plan," Aleck agreed solemnly.

She rolled her eyes. "Whatever. I already know everything anyway." She turned away and skipped toward the kitchen. "Later. I want steak."

"She is so funny and sweet," Delonna said softly. "I see so much of Ian in her."

"Aye," Aleck agreed, once again all broody. "But she's much prettier than him."

"I can't disagree. Want me to hold Ben again so you can go grab food?"

He shook his head. "No, I want you to go find Colin and show him that message. I'll spend a few minutes with the babe and be in shortly."

She sighed and gave a terse nod. "I will."

"And dish me up a plate and save me a spot at the table. Emily will likely clear out half the food before I get in there."

"She's a tiny thing, I can't imagine she'd eat much."

He snorted. "Just you wait and see. She's the size of her mother with the appetite of her da."

"Well then, guess I'd better grab us food."

"Find Colin first."

She nodded and shared a look with him that set her heart beating, before making her way to the kitchen.

So full.

Delonna leaned back in her chair and placed her hand over her stomach. She eyed the last couple bites of steak and baked potato on her plate and regretted leaving them behind. Because everything at dinner had been amazing.

She'd shown Colin the message and he'd written down the info and promised to pass it on to the detectives on the case. She'd be contacted soon, he'd said. She was getting pretty chummy with the Island County Sheriff's Department.

"How'd you like the salad?" Aleck asked, nodding to her plate.

She could still taste the hint of feta from it. "Amazing. Kudos to whoever made it."

"That'd be me." He gave a smug grin.

"Ah, the hell it would," Ian called out, overhearing their conversation. "Steal my credit, will you? The man brought a bag of pre-washed lettuce. I provided all the delicious bits."

She nudged Aleck in the side. "I see what you did there. Your salad-making talents are about equivalent to mine, boss boy."

He made a face and stabbed another piece of steak with his fork. "I'll take that as a compliment."

"As if your ego needs another one," Kenzie teased.

Delonna relaxed in her chair, watching the easygoing banter that went on at the table among the group. She'd known the McLaughlin siblings were close, but any time she spent moments with them like this, it was clear just how much so.

Family was everything to them. They were so utterly tight knit and protective of each other. Not just each other, but those they cared about. That concern and protection had spilled over to Delonna now. And she couldn't begin to express how much she appreciated it.

Even with all that was going on, the violence that had taken over her life, she couldn't deny that she felt much safer when she was with them. Most especially with Aleck.

She noted the conversation turning to the siblings' parents and her ears pricked up at the mention of the dad recovering from surgery.

"What's this I missed?" she asked mildly.

Kenzie glanced her way and sighed. "Da has had hip surgery."

"Aye, and Ma had no intention of telling us, if you can believe it," Colin muttered.

"Oh, I'm sorry." Delonna reached for her beer. "How is your mom holding up?"

"Not so well," Aleck replied, any trace of humor vanishing now. "She says she's fine, but it's just her taking care of Da and it's become clear she's not able to go to work."

"Oh, right. Because all you kids are here." Delonna nodded. "No family over there to help?"

Ian sighed. "We have a cousin nearby, but he's busy with a wife and newborn. Which is why one of us will be flying out to Edinburgh soon."

"If we hadn't just had Ben, we'd go," Sarah said regretfully, glancing over to where the newborn slept in his father's arms.

"Aye, it'd be a bit much to juggle," Aleck agreed, lips twitching in amusement. "Both Da and my nephew would likely give you a bit of fuss."

"Absolutely," Kenzie agreed. "Da is a wonderful man until he gets sick, then he's a grumpy bear. He's quite independent, and I'm sure is not happy being laid up from surgery. Ma is likely having a devil of a time."

"Aye she is." Aleck nodded, looking distracted, maybe off

in his own thoughts.

"I've put in the request for time off," Colin said, leaning back in his chair, his brows furrowing, "and I'm hoping for the best, but I've just been assigned a new case—"

"You should stay," Kenzie waved off the rest of whatever he'd been about to say. "You've a pregnant wife and leaving the country should be the last thing on your mind."

All eyes swung to Hailey and mouths gaped.

Hailey looked just as stunned and her gaze swung to Colin. "I didn't tell anyone."

He shook his head. "Nor I. We only just took a test and received the confirmation. How the bloody hell did you know she was pregnant, Kenzie?"

"Well I didn't until you just told me. It was a lucky guess." Kenzie grinned. "The other morning at breakfast Hailey looked a bit sick and picked at her food. Just a minute ago she was sorting through nuts with the determination of a woman in the throes of a pregnancy craving." She shrugged innocently. "And I knew you guys were trying to have a baby. So like I said: lucky guess."

"So it would seem," Colin murmured.

"All I wanted were the cashews," Hailey blurted. "Crap, I knew I'd do a terrible job hiding it, Colin."

"It was a secret?" Delonna asked, glancing at the two.

"Aye, somewhat. We meant to keep it quiet for a bit." Colin scowled. "Just until she was through the first trimester."

"Sorry, like I said, wild guess. Didn't actually think I'd be right." Kenzie grimaced. "Er, congratulations, though?"

There was a flurry of congratulations and conversation about Hailey's pregnancy, momentarily distracting everyone from the topic that had been at hand.

After offering an encouraging response as well, Delonna leaned back and looked around the table. Aleck had gone quiet again, his brows drawn into a frown. His gaze slid to hers and she saw a moment's calculation that sent a shiver through her.

There was a brief silence around the table.

"I'll go to Edinburgh."

Now all attention shifted to Aleck.

"You'll go?" Kenzie repeated. "But the pub—"

"Will likely be shut down for several days anyway as the repairs are made and the police investigation is ongoing," Aleck explained calmly. "And Kenzie, you're quite able to run things when we do reopen. That is if you're comfortable doing so?"

"I've done it before when you've gone on holiday." She gave a brief nod. "I can handle it fine."

Delonna's heart had started a slow thud. Aleck was going to Scotland, and relatively soon it sounded like. Meaning she was going to be back in her own home, on her own. Without him.

It wasn't so much the fear for her safety that bothered her, but the idea that he'd be an ocean away. Which was stupid. How selfish was she to be slightly disappointed by this news?

Her throat went tight, and she found herself nodding with everyone else.

"Delonna can stay with us, of course," Colin said, glancing her way. "We'll ensure her safety while you're gone. What, a week or so?"

Dismay slid through Delonna. "Oh, there's no need—"

"A week and a half at the most," Aleck continued, ignoring her protest.

His gaze moved to hers, probing and again full of consideration. She couldn't let him feel any guilt or hesitation at going to take care of his parents. She was not a selfish bitch. And she was not that attached to him that she couldn't handle some time apart.

"And there's no need to have Delonna stay with you, Colin," Aleck said softly.

"She could stay here with us?" Sarah volunteered. "If she doesn't mind a fussy newborn."

"She'll not be staying with any of you." Aleck's gaze never left hers. "She's coming to Scotland with me."

Chapter Twelve

MAYBE HE SHOULD'VE spoken to her about it first, Aleck acknowledged silently as they drove back to his place after dinner. Delonna sat fuming next to him, not having said a word since leaving Sarah and Ian's house.

"I can't actually force you to come, you realize," he said reluctantly.

"No, you sure can't."

"But you've admitted you'd love to travel to Scotland."

"Yes, at some point in my life, Aleck." She gave a disbelieving laugh. "I didn't mean next week. And what if I didn't have a passport?"

"But you've already admitted you do."

"Yes. But—"

"What's holding you back?"

She opened her mouth, but hesitated, and so he jumped on it.

"Have I not said I'd cover your airfare with my airline miles? That we've a place to stay there?"

"I can't take that much time off of work!"

"The pub will be closed for several days, anyway, Lana. And I'll pay you for those days, as well as any other shifts that you would've worked."

"Which is extremely generous of you," she acknowledged. "But the hourly wage isn't what pays my bills. It's the tips."

"Aye, and I realize that. You must look at the trade-off, though," he urged. "It's a chance to travel to Scotland."

When she was silent, he cast her another glance and saw the wistful expression on her face.

"You know you'd like to go, luv. And besides, if you're with me, I can keep you safe."

She gave a not-so-silent harrumph. "Your whole family has promised the same thing. All you McLaughlins seem to be sworn protectors."

"It's in our blood. Though, I'd prefer to be the one to do the protecting." He paused and couldn't resist a lopsided smile. "Besides, none of my family offers the bed-sharing benefit."

That made her laugh and his smile grew.

"I see, so this boils down to sex?"

"No, but you can't argue that it's a perk."

"You'll miss me if I don't go," she murmured.

That stole any witty response from him. He settled for honesty. "Aye."

He pulled into his driveway, parked the car and turned to face her.

"I know this seems crazy and it's absolutely impulsive, but I'd love to know you were with me and safe." He caught her hand and threaded his fingers through it. "You'll love Scotland."

She just stared at him and then bit her lip. She shook her head.

"Please. Just say yes, Lana."

Again, no answer, but her fingers tightened around his.

"Just say yes..."

DELONNA SLEPT SO soundly, looking lovely—even with a bit of drool in the corner of her mouth—that Aleck would've given anything for a few more minutes before having to wake her. Unfortunately, that wasn't an option.

He touched her shoulder, leaned over and murmured, "Time to wake up, luv. We've landed and you're in Scotland now."

It took a moment before her lashes fluttered up and her unfocused gaze turned to face him. It had to be the melatonin she'd taken to help her sleep.

"But we can't be," she protested, still half out of it. "I just fell asleep."

"Aye, six hours ago." He reached past her to push open the shade. "Welcome to Edinburgh."

Her gaze swung to glance out the window and she made a soft noise of surprise. The plane was still taxiing toward their gate.

"Ohmygod. It's beautiful. I can tell from here."

He laughed. The most she might be able to see was some green hills off in the distance.

"It's weird. I've never been out of the country before except for Canada, but that doesn't really count."

"Of course not," he murmured.

It had never failed to amuse him that many folks from in and around the Seattle area barely considered Canada international, because they were so close to the border.

Delonna turned back to face him. "Thank you for talking me into coming. I can't even tell you how excited I am to—" she broke off to yawn "—be here."

He touched her cheek and winked. "Maybe even a bit more when you're fully awake, aye?"

"Aye." She smiled. "I'm going to pick up a bunch of Scottish mannerisms, I bet."

"Undoubtedly."

It really hadn't taken much to talk her into it. A couple days of leaving printed images of Scotland around the house. Having bagpipe music playing from his computer. Walking around in his kilt and nothing else—though that had led straight to the bedroom.

And finally she'd given in and agreed to make the trip with him. He'd watched her excitement grow with every moment 'til the plane had taken off. Seeing her eyes alight now, he knew he'd made the right choice. She'd be safe with him. And that was his main reason for bringing her, or so he told himself.

Within an hour they'd gotten off the plane and passed through customs. As they made their way to baggage, he thought to prepare her again.

"My mother will be picking us up."

"I remember." She nodded. "It's really nice of her. I rarely do airport pickups for people, unless I owe them big time."

He grimaced "Right. Well, I meant that more as a warning. My ma is quite—"

"Aleck, my darling boy!" His mother's voice rang through the baggage claim area. "You've come home."

The rushing feet behind him had him and Delonna turning around.

She was an older version of Kenzie, beautiful and full of energy, and about to fling herself into his arms. He dropped his carry-on just in time to welcome her.

His heart expanded with love, his chest with a ragged breath as he wrapped his arms around the petite woman.

"I've missed ya, Ma." He squeezed her, kissing the top of her head.

"Me too, Son."

She squeezed him back, with a strength that was a bit shocking for such a small woman. Her grip relaxed some and she finally stepped away, peeking around him.

"And you've brought your girlfriend after all, aye?"

He winced as she pushed past him.

"Give us a kiss, Delonna."

He tried to meet Delonna's gaze and give her a silent apology, but Delonna was all smiles as his mother gave her a huge hug and kiss on the cheek.

"Lovely to see you in person this time, my dear."

"Nice to see you too, Mrs. McLaughlin." Delonna hugged her back.

"Please, just call me Brenda."

Delonna looked confused for a moment, but then nodded. "All right. I'm sorry to hear your husband if having such a hard time."

"Och, he's a bloody bear with this recovery." His mother pulled away and grimaced. "I'm glad you ignored my protests and came to help anyway. I tell you, the first thing I'm going to do is go have meself a pint and leave you with your da."

Aleck laughed. "And I'll not blame you one bit. You deserve a break."

"Don't I ever." She glanced at him and Delonna. "Well now, let's find your luggage and be on our way."

~

ON THE DRIVE from the airport, Delonna was vaguely aware of the chatter between mother and son, but her attention was more focused on the scenery outside her window.

She was in Scotland. *Scotland.* It seemed surreal and

completely overwhelming, but in a wonderful way. Even though she'd slept a good amount on the plane ride over, she was still pretty exhausted.

Her mind screamed that it was morning here, but her body was in denial, figuring it was still the middle of the night.

"Now we'll get you two settled into your flat," Brenda said, "then you can come have dinner with us."

"Our own flat?" Delonna shot Aleck a questioning look. She'd been under the impression they were staying with his parents.

"Oh aye," Aleck's mom continued. "You'll not want to stay with us—our place is quite messy right now. The flat you both will stay in belonged to Aleck's grandparents. Before they passed away six years ago, my father-in-law made it clear the flat was to be left to the grandchildren so they would have a place to stay anytime they visited."

Delonna stared at Aleck, seeing the faint smile and fondness in his eyes.

"How very generous of them."

"Very much so. They loved their grandchildren. And we love that there's a set place for our children to stay when they visit."

Delonna recalled the story of how Aleck's parents had met. Very sweet, really. His mom, who was an American, had been backpacking through Europe and had met Rodrick McLaughlin. They'd fallen in love, eventually married, and she'd moved to Scotland.

At some point they'd moved to America with their children, opening McLaughlin's Pub on Whidbey, but then eventually the aging couple had moved back to Scotland. All the kids had stayed in the States, and Aleck had taken over the pub. It was just as successful now as it had been when it opened.

Some of the sights outside her car window began to look familiar from the pictures she'd seen online. From the stunning, stone medieval-looking buildings and narrow streets, to what appeared to be Edinburgh Castle at the top of a large, rocky area.

It took her breath away and her pulse pounded a little faster. She was in Scotland. The thought wouldn't stop resonating in her head. If someone had told her last week that she'd be here today, she would've laughed her ass off.

"And here we are," Aleck's mom announced.

A few minutes later they were climbing up the stairs of an older building. Brenda paused outside the door to the second level.

"You've got your keys to the flat, Aleck?"

"Aye, Ma."

"Get yourself settled and come down and see us soon, all right?"

"Will do." He kissed his mother on the cheek and then began ascending the stairs again, carrying both his and Delonna's suitcases.

"Which floor are we on?" she asked. "And here, let me carry my own case, Aleck."

"I've got it. And we're just the next one." He paused on the next landing and she opened the door for them to the hallway.

They shuffled inside and moved in the dimness to the end of the hall. He unlocked the door and gestured for her to go inside.

She stepped in and caught her breath as she glanced around what seemed to be the living room. The hardwood floors were shiny and sanded, the walls a soft eggshell white, and the cushiony couch and oversized chairs were a rich brown. Though it was clearly a smaller home, the layout made it appear spacious, clean and inviting.

"Bedroom is off to the right. I'll drop our cases in there."

She was tempted to follow him to see the room, but the view from the living room window had her veering that way instead. At the window she pressed her fingers against the cool, dated glass and stared outside.

It was completely different from the trees and water sights of living on an island back home. It was a different kind of beauty. Older buildings, weathered and almost magical in a gothic way. The city seemed to shimmer with a sense of secrets and history.

As she lifted her gaze to the end of all the buildings, she again found herself staring at Edinburgh Castle. So different than any castle she'd imagined, almost like a little cluster of buildings perched dangerously on a rocky hillside.

"I'll take you there sometime this week." Aleck's words caressed her ear as he approached from behind her. His hands went to her hips, pulling her back against him.

"I hope so." She leaned against him, still drowsy from the time change, and kept her gaze on the beauty outside the window. "This city is incredibly beautiful."

"It's not Whidbey Island, but it has its own sort of historic beauty."

"I was just thinking the same thing."

"Mmm. Great minds and all that business."

He kissed the side of her neck and she sighed. "If you start that, then we'll never get down to see your parents."

"Mmm. They'll just assume we're settling in." He slid his hands up to cup her breasts and she moaned softly. "But there's something else I'd like to settle into right now."

She couldn't help but laugh at his cheeseball line, even as she was so tempted to just press herself back into him and surrender to the arousal rising inside her.

"I want to," she murmured, "you know I do. But I don't want to keep your parents waiting after we flew across the globe to help them out."

He nibbled on her ear and then sighed. "You're a good lass."

She turned in his arms and cupped his face. "Oh I'm no lass, I'm all woman." She kissed him slowly. "And later, tonight, I'll remind you of that."

He groaned, tightening his arms around her waist. "Shite, but you drive me a bit mad, luv."

"Well then we're even." She slipped out of his arms. "Hey, so your mom's name is Brenda?"

"Aye."

"Isn't that the same name as that girl Colin—"

"Was once engaged to? Aye. Probably another reason it didn't really work out." Aleck grinned. "Can't quite imagine how that went, calling your mother's name out in bed."

"Okay, that's just gross. I didn't go there."

"No need, I did it for you," he said cheerfully.

"You're so weird." She laughed and went to find the bathroom. "Let me freshen up a bit and we can head down."

~

DINING WITH ALECK'S parents was very much like having a meal with the rest of the McLaughlin siblings. The realization sank in through dinner as they ate and chatted away. Conversation was always fast and entertaining.

"So how is your new hip, Da?" Aleck asked.

"Ah, it's not so bad, Son. Can't complain."

Brenda snorted, rolling her eyes at her husband. "Can't complain, can ye? All you've done is complain."

"Maybe if you wouldn't be pecking around so much like a mother hen—"

"I'll peck all I want, I'm your wife."

Delonna bit her lip to keep from laughing and exchanged an amused glance with Aleck.

Aleck cleared his throat. "Are you up and walking much?"

"Aye. Doctor's orders, of course. Hurts like bloody hell, some moments, but gettin' stronger every day." His dad paused. "You needn't have come, but I'm glad you did, Son."

"I wanted to come," Aleck said quietly. "You'd have done the same. And it was actually a blood match in deciding which of your offspring would make the journey."

"And clearly you won that match, and look, you've even brought a girl." His dad beamed at Delonna.

Awkward. She felt like she was about sixteen years old and getting judged by her prom date's parents.

Aleck looked equally uncomfortable. "I did. Delonna works with me and was in need of a holiday."

His dad cleared his throat. "Oh, aye, of course. So you're...ehm, let's see, you're friends?"

Delonna held her breath. How the hell was he going to answer that? You didn't screw your friends every possible chance. But they weren't a couple, were they? She snuck a glance at Aleck and was stunned to see his neck was turning red. Interesting.

"We're, uh, well we're—"

"Oh for goodness' sake, it's none of our bloody business, Rodrick," Brenda interrupted in exasperation. But then she paused and her gaze swung to Delonna. "That is unless you're about to surprise us with another grandchild?"

Delonna nearly choked on her beef. "What? *No.*"

"Shite, really, Ma?"

"*No*!" Delonna emphasized, a little panicked now.

"I was just askin'," Brenda said innocently, her eyes dancing. "And don't be swearin' at your mother."

Aleck glanced Delonna's way, shooting her a silent apology.

"Well, no need to rush on a baby," Rodrick said cheerfully. "We've got little Ben now to tide us over for a bit. And I cannot wait to meet the little lad on our next trip to the States."

"You'll love him. Your grandson is adorable," Delonna said quickly, latching on to the chance to change the subject from a potential baby in her uterus.

Brenda beamed. "Aye, we've seen him when we had a Skype session with Sarah and Ian last week. He's got the McLaughlin green eyes, he does."

"He really does." Delonna glanced at Aleck. Ben's eyes were the same beautiful shade as his uncle's.

He caught her gaze and her stomach did a little dance as something silent passed between them. There was a shuffle of movement and they both swung their attention to Aleck's dad who struggled to get out of his chair.

"What are you about? We've just sat down," Brenda said in exasperation.

"I need to use the bathroom," he grumbled, a sheen of

sweat breaking out on his brow.

Aleck brushed aside his mother who tried to rise, and moved to his dad's side instead, helping the older man despite the protests.

Delonna watched the two and saw the same stubbornness in father in son. They were similar in not only appearance, but also personality, she'd begun to realize.

She took a moment to glance over Rodrick, and had an idea what Aleck would look like in a good twenty-five years or so. His father must've been around sixty. His hair was mostly gray now, though still held a fair amount of black. His face was weathered, but still handsome. His forehead wrinkled in an area that showed he might be prone to scowling just as much as his son. Though there were lines around his mouth that said he didn't hesitate to laugh as well.

"Be back in a moment," Aleck called out as they disappeared down the hall.

"He's rather good with his father," Brenda murmured.

Delonna nodded. "He is."

"Much more patient than I am."

"Well, you've had a lot on your plate. I'm sure you're much more patient than you give yourself credit for."

Brenda took a sip of the beer in her hand and gave Delonna a considering look. "How long have you known my son?" she asked.

Shifting in her seat, Delonna gave a small smile. "Oh,

well, a few years, I suppose. I've worked at the pub for a while now."

"Aye." Brenda nodded, her speculative gaze missing nothing. "I'm quite surprised he brought you here, honestly."

"I am too. It's not cheap—"

"It's not the money, so much. It's just that you're the first woman I've ever seen Aleck spend any time with besides his sister or sisters-in-law." Brenda paused, her brows drawing together. "There was just Cassie, but that was ages ago."

Cassie? Was this the ex Kenzie had begun to mention last week? The girlfriend from Aleck's past?

Before she could ask, or his mom could elaborate, the men began to return from the bathroom. Delonna could hear the slide of the walker in the hallway.

Brenda stood and went to pull out her husband's chair. Despite all the bickering from earlier, it was sweet to see the kiss she pressed against her husband's temple when he was seated again. And the way he caught her hand and pressed a kiss to the knuckles.

Delonna's heart warmed a little, and she turned her attention back to her food, feeling almost intrusive on the tender moment.

When dinner had ended, they sat in the living room for a bit, chatting, before the evening began to wind up.

"Did you want a break, Ma?" Aleck asked. "We'll stay

with Da if you wanted to head to the pub for a pint?"

Delonna had assumed his mother had been joking, but glancing at Brenda, she saw the other woman was clearly considering it.

"Not tonight, Son," she finally said. "But if you don't mind coming over tomorrow, it'll give me a chance to run to the grocer."

"Of course we will," Delonna answered, before Aleck could. "We'll bring breakfast. Find a bakery with something tasty."

"Oh, if you'd pick up Starbucks, that'd be lovely!" His mother's eyes lit up.

"Starbucks?" Delonna repeated, a little surprised.

"Aye, there's one on the Royal Mile, not far from here. I do enjoy a good mocha."

"Oh, of course. We'll grab some, um, Starbucks."

Delonna couldn't help but smile. She'd come all the way from the Seattle area and her official first breakfast in Scotland was going to be from Starbucks.

"But I'm sorry to say that we're a bit tired tonight," Brenda murmured. "Why don't you kids go out and have some fun. Visit your cousin at his pub."

"Your cousin owns a pub too?" Delonna glanced at Aleck.

"Aye. It's all in the family." He gave a lazy smile. "And I did promise we'd stop by if possible."

"Well I'm game if you are."

"Go," Brenda encouraged. "Have fun."

"Have a pint for me," Rodrick agreed. "Your ma is being quite stingy on allowing me my drink."

"You can't be mixing alcohol with your meds, luv."

"Bah. I'll not believe that for a moment."

"Right, then." Aleck hesitated. "Well, if you're sure you don't mind?"

"Go." Brenda waved them away. "We'll see you in the morning."

Chapter Thirteen

THE PUB, IT turned out, was within walking distance. The autumn night was chilly, but dry fortunately. Really, the climate didn't seem altogether that different from the Pacific Northwest.

Delonna was still drinking it all in, and glanced up in surprise as Aleck caught her hand, lacing his fingers through hers.

"You were quite charming with my parents."

"Was I?"

"Aye."

"Well, they're lovely people."

"They can be obnoxious. Like with that grandchild comment."

"Oh yes." She grinned. "That part where they not-so-tentatively threw out there that you may have knocked me up?"

Aleck didn't smile in response. If anything he seemed a little sobered by the conversation.

"Aye, that part," he muttered. "Sometimes they jump

right over the line of discretion in the sand."

"I completely get it. I have parents too." She squeezed his hand in encouragement as they made their way carefully over the cobbled streets. "So what's your cousin like?"

"Hmm. He's a bit like Kenzie, personality wise, but with a penis." He grinned now. "He's blunt. Funny. Blithe. A nice bloke really. He'll unintentionally insult you at some point tonight."

"I'm not easily insulted." She glanced around the buildings they walked between. At night the old city seemed even more gothic—and haunted maybe. A shiver ran through her, and it wasn't entirely from the cold.

Surprisingly, it was quiet with only a few people out and about, even though it wasn't yet seven.

"Are you tired?" Aleck asked softly.

"No, I've got a second wind now. I'm too excited to be here. And I think I got enough sleep on the flight to hold me a few more hours."

"Me too. Actually, one moment." He stopped suddenly, causing her to nearly stumble on the uneven streets.

"What is it?"

"This." He backed her up against a cold, craggy building and caught her mouth with his own.

Her breath hitched and she looped her arms around his neck, her tongue slipping out to stroke against his. The kiss was lazy and unhurried, as exploratory as it was gentle.

There was something so utterly romantic and whimsical

about kissing someone in a foreign city. Especially a fascinating medieval city like Edinburgh.

When he lifted his head, her heart was skipping a bit quicker and happiness was riding through her blood.

"That was nice," she said softly.

"Aye." He brushed another light kiss against her lips. "I've missed kissing you."

"You kissed me when we arrived at the flat."

"That was this morning." He smiled. "I want you, Lana. And if it wasn't so damn cold, I'd likely take you in one of these wynds."

"What's a wynd?"

"The alleys between these buildings, luv."

"I see. And, no, you wouldn't." She shook her head and drew a finger down his chest. "You'd never risk getting caught breaking the rules. Despite your bad-boy antics, you're a pretty good guy."

"Bad boy, you say?"

"Mmm."

"You think I'm a bad boy?"

"I don't know, would a straight-and-narrow guy screw his employee on the pool table?"

His eyes closed and a shudder ripped through him. "Christ, Lana, I'd rather not go see me cousin with a bloody hard-on."

"Me cousin?" That distracted her. "Off the plane not even a day and your Scottish dialect is already back in full force."

"It tends to do that. And look how brilliantly you changed the subject."

"Well..." She shrugged innocently and glanced down at his crotch. "I was trying to play nice and not get a rise out of you again—"

"Not helping here."

She stood on her tiptoes and nibbled on his earlobe. "Let's go check out your cousin's pub, and I promise to take care of your hard-on later."

"*Lana*," he hissed.

Laughing, she tugged at his hand and they started off down the street again.

~

SHITE, BUT THIS woman kept him on his toes. Kept him always hungry for her, and enjoying life in a way he hadn't in, well, maybe ever.

Aleck led her through the small, quiet streets of Old Town Edinburgh and finally to the pub inside one of the buildings.

Fortunately, the last few minutes—and imagining hairy, mean nuns from his childhood—had brought his erection back under control.

They opened the door to the pub and walked inside, and it was only seconds before they were spotted.

"Aleck McLaughlin." His cousin's voice rang out. "You

doss cunt! Welcome home."

"Did he just call you a cunt?" Delonna whispered, looking stricken. "Because I'm about to be genuinely offended on your behalf."

"Oh, don't be, luv. It's an endearment," he said briskly.

"Seriously?" She shot him a look of disbelief. "What the hell kind of endear—"

"Ted! How the fook are you, Cousin?" Aleck released her hand to give his equally tall and burly relative a hug.

"I'm very weel. Life is good and I can't complain. So good to see you abandon your Yankee life for a bit to come see family." Ted's smile widened as he looked at Delonna. "And who's this lovely lass? You've gone and got yourself a girlfriend, have you?" the man demanded, his gaze sweeping over her. "Not bad. Not bad at all."

Delonna blinked, and then said, "I am right here, you realize."

"Aye, you are. I can't quite stop looking actually. That jumper does lovely things to your—*oof*." He broke off as Aleck smacked him in the back of the head.

Christ, if Delonna had picked up the fact that Ted was about to compliment her breasts, she showed no sign of it. Maybe just a little amused, actually.

"Stop while you're ahead, Ted. It's fookin' good to see you, man. Been far too long. Now pour my arse a whisky. Neat. It's been a long day of travel."

"Not a problem. And you, lass, what'll you have?"

She scanned the menu above the bar. "I'll take one of your ciders, please."

"A cider and whisky for the lovely couple." Ted moved behind the bar and prepared their drinks.

"Not so different than our pub, hmm?" Delonna murmured, glancing around. "Although…Aleck, there are dogs in here."

His lips twitched. "Aye."

"Not like medical dogs, but like regular pets."

"Mmm hmm."

"Do you see that?" She leaned toward him and lowered her voice. "There's a super fat pug that I'm pretty sure is sharing an order of fish and chips with a dude back there."

"Aye, we allow dogs in the pub," Ted said with a grin, returning with their drinks. "It's not so uncommon here, you see."

"Apparently." She took a sip of her cider and made a sound of content. "Even better when you're drinking this while *in* Scotland."

"Not a dog person, is she?" Ted asked Aleck. "More into the cats?"

Aleck shrugged. "I think she swings both ways."

Delonna eyed them both suspiciously. "Did this conversation just get dirty?"

"Dirty?" Ted slid a round glass that matched Aleck's her way. It was filled two fingers high with an amber liquid.

"She's a filthy mind, Ted. Best not go there."

"I do not have a filthy mind," she sputtered, elbowing him in the ribs. "Okay, maybe a little. What is this?" She lifted the glass. "Aleck ordered the whisky, not me."

"Scotch whisky, lass. Highland Park. We're all having a toast."

She raised a brow. "This is classy stuff."

"Aye, only the best for me cousin and his new lass." Ted winked and poured himself a glass. "Cheers, mates."

Aleck lifted his glass. "Cheers."

Delonna echoed the toast and then they all sipped and enjoyed their whisky. No amateur hour of tossing it back like the customers at the pub back on the island.

"That was fantastic." She set the glass down a moment later. "Thank you, Ted."

He nodded. "Glad you liked it."

"And I actually *am* a dog person, so if you'll excuse me, I'm going to go say hello to that pub-crashing pooch."

They watched her stride off and kneel beside the dog, having no problem striking up a conversation with the owner, it seemed.

"Well if she isn't a wee cheeky thing." Ted shook his head. "Pretty as fook too, Cousin."

"Aye."

"You'd better marry her quick, or someone else will."

Aleck froze and he curled his fingers around the empty glass. Why did it always come back to relationships? To marriage? Then again, he shouldn't have expected anything less when he'd brought Delonna to Edinburgh.

He'd never even brought a girl to dinner until last week when Delonna had come along. But then he'd had a reason then. To keep her safe. And that was also the reason he'd brought her to Edinburgh. Well, part of it. The other part was him imagining over a week without her in his bed.

"No marriage," he said with a brief smile. "We're not that serious, really."

"No? You're quite certain?" Ted looked amused now.

"Aye."

"Hmm. Then you'll not mind that Jeffrey seems quite taken with her."

Jeffrey? Aleck swung his attention back to where Delonna seemed more interested in the dog's owner now. She laughed at something he said and pushed her blonde braid over her shoulder, reaching down to pet the dog again.

The bastart Jeffrey kept talking, but Aleck didn't miss the way the man ran an interested gaze over her. Lingering on her large chest that Ted had nearly pointed out earlier as well.

Fook it all.

"She's just the friendly sort," Aleck muttered, trying to keep his words casual.

They were sleeping together—that was it. It shouldn't bother him the least if she chose to flirt with another fellow.

"Aye, I can see just how friendly she is. Chatting with about five blokes now."

The hell she was. Jaw going tight, he reluctantly glanced over his shoulder again. Sure enough, there were six, not five, men crowded around Delonna and laughing. It was as if this Jeffrey wanker had invited his mates over to join the fun.

"How long are you here for?" Ted asked. "Will you have time to drop by and see me family?"

"We're here for just a week, but yes, let Marie know we'd love to come visit."

"She'll be thrilled. Give us a moment, while I help this fella." Ted moved down the bar counter to talk to another customer.

Aleck didn't mind, because it gave him a moment to glance back at Delonna. She was laughing and interacting with the men quite easily. He'd always assumed her friendliness was just part of the job, but clearly her personable chatter went beyond bartending. He shouldn't have been surprised.

As he continued to watch, the bloke who'd just been up at the bar ordering something from Ted returned to the group and handed Delonna a drink.

Another bloody man joining the group and trying to get her tossed. He heard her weak protest, but the man brushed it off, and a moment later she accepted the beer.

"Careful, Aleck, your jealousy is showing."

"Jealous?" He gave a hard shrug. "Delonna's a grown woman, she'll do as she pleases. At the end of the night, I know whose bed she'll be in."

Ted winced. "Och, but that's a bit crass. Even for you."

It was, and he hated that he'd made such a stupid remark aloud. He hated even more that his cousin was right, and he was experiencing a remarkable amount of jealousy for someone he was supposed to just be sleeping with.

His cousin began to whistle, and though not completely familiar with pop music, Aleck was pretty certain he recognized that Beyoncé song about "putting a ring on it" or some such shite.

Scowling, he tapped his glass on the counter and muttered, "Stop winding me up and pour me another one of these, you doss cunt."

His cousin threw back his head, laughed, and then went to grab the whisky.

~

MAYBE SHE SHOULDN'T have accepted that drink from the new guy, Delonna mused.

What was his name? Kevin? She'd drunk the whisky, and then that cider, and now with a beer she was starting to feel really good. Like, really good.

She sat in a chair with the men, listening to them joke and chat. At first she'd felt a bit guilty at not returning to Aleck after going to visit the dog. But when she'd seen him laughing and chatting with Ted, she figured he'd probably want a few minutes to catch up with his cousin.

Besides, these guys here were harmless. Talking about

their dogs, whisky and of course, asking questions about America and how did she like Scotland. Oh she liked it just fine, even though she'd only been here for a half a day and hadn't seen too much.

She didn't mind keeping her dialog light and just listening to them talk though. She could pretty much close her eyes and hear a Scot talk all day. Their accents were fabulous. She told them as much after her third drink.

"We've no accents, you've the accent, lass," one protested with a loud belly laugh.

"Aye," another chimed in. "I knew she was American the moment I heard her at the bar."

"Yes, my apologies." She grinned and rubbed the doggy behind the ears again. The pug had shockingly abandoned his fish and chips in favor of her attention.

It was a different dynamic than the regulars at McLaughlin's Pub. Not that she didn't love McLaughlin's. She did. But there was something a little more down to earth at the pubs around here. Personable.

She was having a blast. Though a quick glance back at the bar counter found Aleck was now watching her, and he didn't seem all too pleased. Maybe it looked bad. Like she had a male harem or something.

"Well, thanks for letting me hang out for a while. I'd better get back to my..." Was she allowed to say boyfriend? Was Aleck her boyfriend?

No, idiot, sleeping with someone does not make them your

boyfriend. You'd need to have "the talk" first.

"Aleck McLaughlin? She's Aleck's girl?" one of the men asked, disappointment lacing his words.

"I'm here with Aleck, yes." It was a safe response.

"Och, there goes any chance you had, Ernie."

As the general ribbing continued, Delonna made her way back to the bar and sat down on the stool next to Aleck.

"Having fun?"

"Yes," she answered, completely honestly. She gave a slow laugh and shook her head. "A hell of a lot of fun, actually. I love it here. You run a fantastic pub, Ted."

"I do, don't I?" Ted grinned and slid a—crap, another one?—cider her way.

"The energy in this pub is incredible. These locals are so friendly."

"It's no' so different than yours, aye?" Ted asked Aleck.

"They have their similarities," Aleck agreed. "We're a bit more unforgiving on the no dogs rule."

"You guys have the best job in the world—owning a pub. I can't wait until I can say the same."

"You want to open a pub?" Ted asked.

She froze, realizing what she'd said. She'd never mentioned her dream to Aleck, but the cat was out of the bag and she saw no use in hiding it now.

"Yes," she admitted hesitantly. "I mean, someday."

There was silence to her right, and she snuck a glance over to find Aleck's brows drawn together.

"You'll open a pub of your own?" Aleck repeated.

"Pub or bar. Something of the sort. I can't pull off the Scottish thing." She gave a nervous laugh. He wasn't smiling. "The McLaughlins pretty much staked that niche market on the island."

He looked flat-out distressed now. "You'll be leaving me."

"Not you, the pub," she teased gently. Clearly he was just worried about losing his best bartender. "And this isn't anytime soon, this is a someday thing. It's one reason I've been so careful saving money. I wanted to find a location to lease and get the ball rolling."

He didn't look reassured. "Are you not happy working for me?"

"Right then. A customer is waving me down," Ted said with a forced laugh. "I'll be back, oh, how about when this awkward little moment is over?"

Alone now, Delonna turned to face Aleck. "I love working for you. I love being a bartender. I've told you that."

His jaw flexed and clearly he was struggling with his temper. "You enjoy working for me, so I fail to see the problem."

"Well, *there* is the problem," she tried to explain. "I don't want to just be an employee anymore—I want to have the place be mine. To have a stake in it. I want more than just saying I work as a bartender at a pub, I want it to be my home away from home."

"Does it not feel like home? My pub?"

"It does," she agreed with a small smile. "But that's just it. It's not mine to feel that way about. It's yours. And I'll just be Delonna, the bartender, easily fired if you get the whim to do so."

His gaze darkened. "I'd never fire you on a whim, Lana. You know that."

"I do." Her heart ached for a moment and she took another swig of cider. "Because I'm your best damn bartender."

"Aye, you are, but that's not why. I'm not a complete bastart, luv. You'll always have a job for as long as you'll need it." He sighed and shook his head. "But if your dream is to have your own pub, then I can understand that."

A bit of relief slid through her. "Can you?"

"Aye. It's what I wanted as well at your age."

Your age. Like she was some damn kid. God it pissed her off when he spoke to her that way.

"It's why my parents let me take over their pub." He met her gaze. "You realize it's a lot of responsibility."

"I know. I've seen how the weight of it on your shoulders can nearly bring you to your knees some days."

He smiled faintly and caught her hand. "You keep me on my feet, though."

"You're going to be so screwed when I leave." She'd meant the line to be flippant and cute, but it was somewhat heavy and depressing.

As much as she'd dreamed about opening her own place,

she didn't want to think about leaving McLaughlin's Pub right now. It symbolized her entire world. It meant leaving Aleck. The idea of that last one stung more than it should've.

A lively song came on in the pub and despite the fact that no one was dancing, she grabbed his hand and pulled him to his feet.

"What are you about?" he demanded, though he didn't protest as she dragged him to the small area that might've been a dance floor. Or maybe just where live music usually played on the weekends.

"Dance with me."

"You realize they're playing this song for you, lass. Having a bit of sport." He wrinkled his nose. "You'll not usually hear bagpipes in a pub as background music."

"Does it matter? I'm doing the Highland Fling. It's a dance, you know. Kenzie showed it to me."

Aleck gave a loud, booming laugh. "That is not how I recall the Highland Fling."

"You kick your legs." She kicked a leg. "You shake your ass."

"Fairly certain shaking your arse is *not* part of one of our traditional dances."

"Maybe not." She grinned. "But it works. Don't you think?" She wiggled her butt and then kicked her legs. "Join me, boss boy."

"It's a solo dance, luv, but I'm in no mind to let you do it alone right now. You'd probably fall down. I believe you're drunk."

Her mouth gaped and she stopped dancing momentarily. "Take that back. I'm not drunk."

"Shall I have you walk a straight line?"

She pursed her lips, seriously considering it. "I'd rather keep dancing."

He grimaced. "Be that as it may, I'm no' much for dancin'."

"I'll dance with you, dear." The dog owner from earlier joined them on the floor. "And I'll show you the proper way to do the Highland Fling."

She glanced at Aleck, certain he might have something to say about the interruption, but despite the slight tightening of his mouth, he made no move to stop them.

Fine. It wasn't like she could just be rude.

"All right then," she said and gave the other man a friendly smile. "Show me how it's done, Jeffrey."

Chapter Fourteen

BY THE TIME they stumbled into the flat, it was nearly midnight. While Delonna was singing and laughing her way into the bathroom, he was struggling with a surly temper that had pretty much kicked in when Delonna had become the darling of the pub.

Once good old Jeffrey had danced with her, the men had lined up to take a turn teaching Delonna various forms of Scottish dancing. He'd wanted her to turn them down. Had no right to ask her to turn them down, but he'd wanted her to.

She came out of the bathroom a moment later, her grin even wider.

"I'm not a lightweight, but you were right, Aleck." She poked a finger in the middle of his chest. "I think I'm a little drunk."

"A little," he agreed. She wasn't completely pissed, but definitely was on the happier side of sober.

"You know what I'd like now, Mr. McLaughlin?" She stepped closer and wrapped her arms around his neck.

He had a fair good idea, but asked anyway, "What would you like?"

She stood on her toes and kissed his lips. "I'd veeery much like it if you'd make love to me now."

"That sounds fantastic, but I wouldn't want to take advantage, luv." But he did. He really did. Especially when he was still irritated at the thought of all those bloody wankers dancing with her.

"It's not like my virtue is in danger," she teased.

"You're right." He lifted her off her feet and she gave a squeal of surprise as he carried her to the bedroom. "All gentlemanly intentions are now cast aside and you should prepare yourself to be thoroughly shagged."

"So much talk, so little action." She giggled and touched his stubbly cheek. He hadn't shaved since they'd flown out yesterday.

"I'll show you action," he muttered, depositing her on the bed.

He climbed on next to her, so they were both kneeling on the mattress. After grabbing her sweater, she tugged it up and over her head.

"You were quite popular tonight," he murmured.

"Your parents seemed to like me."

"I didn't mean my parents." He knew his words had an edge to them, and prayed she hadn't noticed.

"Oh, the guys at the bar?" She reached out to pull his shirt off in return. "What can I say? I'm a people person."

"I know. You bring in a shite-ton of customers at McLaughlin's." He unfastened her bra and tossed it aside.

"Again, I think it's my tits."

He groaned, unable to look away. He managed a hoarse, "It could be the tits."

"Touch them," she commanded, her lashes fluttering closed.

He reached out to cup the weight of their discussion in his hands, loving the fullness of them and watching the pink tips tighten. He dipped his head, drawing one nipple into his mouth. Her sigh of pleasure turned into a moan when he sucked harder.

"Don't stop," she whispered. "It feels so good."

Stopping hadn't even crossed his mind, but getting his fingers into her knickers had.

He unfastened her jeans, not about to abandon the sweet nipple in his mouth, and then eased his hand inside. He pushed past the soft cotton and found warm, moist flesh.

She gasped and her legs shifted, opening her body to him. He used the invitation to slide a finger into her heat.

Every man in the pub tonight had watched Delonna. Damn near lining up to chat with her. Dance with her. Be in her presence. Partly, he knew, it was the novelty of having an American lass in a pub that was less touristy, and more locals.

More so, he acknowledged she was just charming as fook. She was young, full of energy and an absolute stunner. She had the curves of a pinup girl, and a sexy laugh and smile that drew the attention of any straight man with a pulse.

But she was here with him now. None of those wankers had taken her home. She was with him. In his arms and crying out, whispering *his* name when he reached up to rub her clit.

Before she could come, he pulled his finger from her body and deftly pushed her back onto the mattress. He pulled off the rest of her clothes in record time, tossing them to the side, and then did the same with his.

Soon he was back, burying his face between her legs with the determination to make her forget about any other bloke.

She seemed almost startled by how fiercely he claimed her with his mouth, but her shocked gasp soon turned to moans. She gripped his hair, riding his tongue.

"Aleck," she whispered. "Oh God. *Yes.*"

He caught her arse in his hands, pulling her snug against his mouth to taste her deeper. To lash at her clit until she was screaming and falling apart in his arms. With her body still shaking from climax, he moved up her body, positioned himself between her legs and drove himself inside her.

She clutched his shoulders and wrapped her legs around his waist. Her hips rose to meet each thrust, her passion equally frenzied.

He took her hard, until she cried out with each thrust deep into her. His mind was only on her and the complete, primal instinct that had taken over.

"Lana," he rasped. "Look at me."

She moaned, her eyes still closed, her nails dragging down his back as he continued to move inside her.

"Look at me," he commanded again, pausing to catch her wrists and pin her arms above her head.

Her lashes fluttered up and the hazel eyes that were glassy and unfocused with passion finally showed a flicker of awareness.

He pushed slow and deep into her, holding her gaze. "You're mine."

A shiver racked her body and surprise shone in her eyes now.

"Mine," he said again, easing out of her tightness. "Say it."

"Yes." She didn't try to free her wrists and her eyes glittered now with comprehension. "Yours. I don't want anyone else."

Her words snapped his last shred of control and he moved deep into her with a roar. He rode her fast and hard, until she couldn't keep up but her body moved only by the force of his thrusts alone.

His body tightened with the anticipation of release. He clasped her wrists harder, using his other arm to hold himself above her.

"Lana." Her name, fevered and hoarse, spilled from his lips as he came.

His arm gave out and he fell on top of her. Everything

was a muddle of sensation and pleasure. Of beating hearts that seemed to be in unison. She kissed his shoulder, smoothing her hand down his back.

"Damn," he said weakly, trying to get his breath back. To orient himself with reality.

"It's okay."

He heard her words. They seemed far away, as if they were from the other end of a tunnel.

"I'm on birth control."

Birth control. What was she about? He lifted his head and stared down at her, trying to get his gaze and thoughts to focus.

It's okay.

Shite. They hadn't used a condom. How the fook had he allowed himself not to use protection?

"You're sure?" His words were sluggish, as if he were the one a bit buzzed.

"Yes. I've been on it for a year. And I was tested recently and I'm fine. I may have been on the pill, but I made James use a condom." She gave a self-conscious laugh and rubbed her hand over his neck. "And isn't this a romantic discussion."

No, it wasn't. The last person Aleck wanted to think about at this moment was James.

"I've never been without a condom," he said numbly. Though one had broken before. "I don't quite know what just happened and how I could've forgotten."

"I do." Her smile was slow and sensual. "I just had the best sex of my life. And I'm pretty sure you did too." She arched a brow. "Unless I'm being presumptuous?"

"No. You're not." That was the bloody crazy thing about it. She was dead-on.

He eased his weight off her and she immediately slid out of the bed.

"Be right back," she said softly, before making her way to the bathroom.

Aleck rolled onto his back and stared at the ceiling, trying to dissect all the crazy emotions going on in his head.

When Delonna returned moments later and crawled into bed, she snuggled up against him. He slid his arm around her and pulled her close, realizing he'd missed the warmth of her in just those few moments.

Tonight was no different than any other night they'd had sex, he told himself. Nothing had changed. Nothing would change.

He pulled the blankets over their shoulders, kissed her forehead, and tried not to overthink things.

~

"CAN I GET you some more tea, Mr. McLaughlin?"

"Thanks, m'dear, but I'm fine."

Delonna nodded and joined Rodrick McLaughlin in the living room. The television was on, airing some show that must've been a UK thing, because she didn't recognize it.

Brenda had run to the grocery as promised, and Aleck was in the kitchen preparing lunch for his dad.

"You adjusting well to the time change?" Rodrick asked, glancing at her.

"For the most part. I'm a little tired, but I think that's more from having a late night."

A late night of spectacular sex. Knowing Aleck's dad was watching her had her willing her face not to turn red.

Aleck had been surprisingly normal this morning. He hadn't acknowledged once what had happened during their crazy lovemaking last night.

Crazy intense.

Her heart beat a little fast just from thinking about how Aleck had been...the things he'd said.

You're mine.

She'd agreed. It hadn't been the alcohol talking. It hadn't been the passion. She'd looked into his eyes and had realized the truth. It had never been this way with any other guy, and she wasn't sure she ever wanted it to be again. Right now, she was his.

"How was the pub last night then?" Rodrick asked.

She smiled, grateful for the distraction Aleck's dad offered. "It was fabulous. Such a fun little place. We had a great time."

Aleck entered the room with a tray in his hands and she noticed him scowling. At least *she'd* had fun. Maybe Aleck hadn't enjoyed it as much.

"You McLaughlins seem to have nailed this pub thing. I hope I do half as well when I open one someday."

"Ah, you want to open a pub, do ya?" Rodrick asked, his expression lighting.

"Someday," she murmured.

"Your lunch, Da." Aleck set the food down on the small table near his dad.

"There's no curry sauce on this chicken?"

"Ma specifically said you're supposed to have it plain. No salt. No sauce."

"Bah. She's no' a doctor!"

"Aye, weel your blood pressure is getting a wee bit high, Da. Stop fussin' and eat the bland bird."

Delonna's lips twitched as she fought a smile. There it was again. Aleck's thickening accent. Good thing they were only here for a bit, or soon she'd lose all ability to understand him. There'd been a couple men at the pub last night where listening to them had been like trying to decipher another language.

"Aye? Well maybe you should have a new hip put in and tell me how your blood pressure is farin'."

"Christ, Ma was right. You are an ornery patient," Aleck grumbled.

"And don't I know it," his dad groused in return. He took the tray and sighed. "I'm a complete arse, Son, and I'll own up to it. So please accept me apology and me thanks for all you've done. But for fook's sake, allow a man his dignity to be in a shite mood."

Aleck laughed. "Have at it. Be as cranky as you'd like, and I'll no' tell Ma."

Delonna smiled, watching the exchange with open amusement and fascination. What a fun, healthy relationship they had.

"How's the chicken?" Aleck asked once his father had taken a bite.

"Bland as hell, but I suppose it'll do."

"Good. Try your juice, you may find it more to your liking."

Delonna shot Aleck a suspicious look as Rodrick eagerly reached for his juice and took a sip.

His dad's face lit up. "Ye've put whisky in."

"Just a splash."

Delonna smacked Aleck's shoulder. "Seriously? Your mother said he wasn't supposed to mix alcohol and meds."

"It wasn't even a half a shot. He'll be fine, and it's no' as if he's drivin' anywhere." Aleck grinned, but ducked his head and looked like a guilty schoolboy. "But don't tell me ma, or she'll box me upside the head."

Delonna didn't doubt it for a moment. When the door to the flat opened a moment later, she had to turn away to hide any guilty expression.

"How are all me lovelies getting on?" Brenda asked, sweeping into the living room.

"Just fine, Ma." Aleck kissed his mother on the cheek.

"How was the supermarket?"

"As relaxin' as a holiday. I stopped at the pub on the way there and had that pint."

"Starting early, I see," Aleck teased.

"Can you blame me?" She moved to kiss her husband on the cheek. "Have you been difficult, my luv?"

"No more than usual." Rodrick grinned and took a sip of juice.

Brenda eyed the barely touched chicken and then glanced at the half-empty juice. She took the glass from her husband's hand, sniffed it and then took a sip.

She set it back down, turned to Aleck and cuffed him upside the head.

Delonna couldn't stop her choked laugh.

"I see what you did there with his juice," Brenda grumbled, but made no move to take the drink from her husband.

"Och, really, Ma?" Aleck winced, but clearly it was more from embarrassment.

"Aye, really." She waved her hand at him. "Now why don't you kids go have fun and see the city? I've had me break for the day and can take care of your da."

"Are you sure?" Aleck asked. "We're here for you."

"And you've already been a tremendous help. Take your girl and have fun."

It didn't matter how often Aleck had told them they weren't a couple, his parents weren't buying it. Delonna just rolled with it now, and Aleck had stopped denying it. It didn't even seem to faze him much anymore.

"Have him take you to the castle, lass," Brenda said turning to her.

"Don't do the castle," Rodrick muttered, sipping on his juice. "It's expensive and glorified. If you look, you'll find plenty of free things to see about town."

Brenda made a noise of disbelief. "Ya thrifty little bugger, you've seen it before and of course it's a waste of your money. Let the girl see the castle. They're not exactly on every corner of America, now are they?"

"I'll take her to the castle and up the Royal Mile," Aleck promised, moving to her side.

"Though we did see some of it this morning when we stopped at Starbucks to bring you breakfast," Delonna added.

"Ah that was so lovely of you. Though nothing would've been open yet, aye?"

"No, not much was open," Delonna agreed. Still, sitting in a Starbucks that looked out over a medieval city had been pretty freaking amazing.

"Weel go see the city now while the shops are still open and there's daylight."

~

NOT LONG AFTER, Delonna found herself strolling up the Royal Mile toward the castle, holding Aleck's hand.

"I'm in love with this city," she confessed. "The shops.

The history—"

"Some of that history is quite dark."

"Isn't that the case with most places?" She shook her head. "It's beautiful. That cathedral we went into—St. Giles, was it?—is almost a thousand years old, Aleck. It took my breath away."

"It's lovely," he agreed. "I've always found it fascinating."

She squeezed his hand and he looked down, and they shared a brief, intimate glance.

"I'm glad you like it here," he said softly. "You're up for the walk to the castle?"

"It's not far at all, and I really would love to see it." She looked up the slightly inclining street they walked along, known as the Royal Mile, which led directly to the castle.

Truth be told, she was a little sore from last night's intense, frenzied lovemaking, but she wasn't about to admit that to him. It was her delicious little secret. Besides, the walking was working out her achy muscles.

By the time they reached the castle and had paid for tickets, she was full of energy and excitement.

"How many times have you been here? Honestly?" She glanced at Aleck.

"Too many times to count." He grinned. "But all the better to show you the fun stuff."

And he did. Or at least the areas of the castle that were open to the public. She was most fascinated by St. Margaret's Chapel, which was the oldest part of the castle. It was small and, as Aleck had told her, the only thing Robert the Bruce hadn't had destroyed hundreds of years ago when he'd captured the castle.

Also fascinating was the Great Hall and the National War Museum of Scotland. There was just so much to see and she drank it all in eagerly, taking picture after picture with her phone.

"It reminds me of Fort Casey, a little," she told him as they stood on one of the perimeter walls. Fort Casey, a military fort on Whidbey, wasn't nearly as old, maybe a century.

"Some parts of it, aye," Aleck agreed.

The wind whipped over the walls of the castle, and she knew they should probably go back down to where it was more sheltered, but she wanted a few more minutes to take it all in. To imprint this moment in her mind forever.

"I know I sound like a broken record, but this is amazing." She leaned back against him.

His arms tightened around her waist and he rested his chin on her head as they stared out over the city together.

"It's magical."

"It is." He kissed the top of her head and her stomach got all warm and tingly.

She closed her eyes, and leaned back into his arms. The magic of the city put her completely at peace, almost in another realm. She'd never felt so protected. So content. So absolutely connected to another person.

With the strong, stone castle walls surrounding her, the not-so-solid wall around her heart began to crack. She wanted to let down her defenses. Throw caution to the wind that whipped around them.

"Aleck," she said softly, not taking her eyes off the view.

"Mmmm?"

"I think I might be falling in love with you."

He didn't say anything, but he went still behind her. She could feel the tension in his body now. Was he even breathing? Maybe she should have kept that caution away from the wind.

He finally gave a slight, forced-sounding laugh. "Then, if I might suggest, maybe you could get your lovely arse back up?"

Chapter Fifteen

WHAT THE HELL had made him say it? His light, teasing reply had become anything of the sort.

She jerked out of his arms a moment later and turned to face him. Shock and a bit of disbelief flashed across her face.

"Get back up?" she repeated unsteadily. "I say that I might be falling in love with you, and you tell me to get back up?"

"Aye," he said with a pathetic attempt at a smile. "It's a play on the falling part, you see—"

"Oh, I get it, Aleck." She wrapped her arms around her chest, looked at him for a moment and then turned away. "What the hell is wrong with you?"

A group of tourists passing by glanced their way and Aleck moved closer to her.

"Perhaps we should go back to the flat," he said quietly. "Talk there."

"Perhaps I should just go back to your cousin's pub and get shitfaced. Because I'm not sure I can handle this conversation sober. I was an idiot to start it."

He shook his head, trying to figure out how the hell to handle this. "You don't need a drink, Lana."

"I need something." She moved away from him, walking down the stairs and off the castle walls.

She made her way back toward the entrance of the castle, moving so fast he had to nearly run to catch up with her.

"Lana."

She didn't even slow her pace. If anything she quickened it as she left the castle and made her way back down the Royal Mile.

"Stop. Delonna, *stop*." He caught her arm and forcibly halted her on the cobbled street, turning her around to face him. "I fooked up."

Anger flashed on her face now. "You really did."

"I didn't know how to reply."

"Well, if you loved me, I'm guessing you would've said something like, 'Hey, cool, me too.' Or something along those lines. But because you told me to *get my ass back up*, that's pretty much anti-being-in-love."

He was a bloody bastart. He knew it. He shook his head, struggling for the words to explain.

"But even if it's not love, and you're not sure how to respond, you could've just kissed me and left it at that." Her eyes flashed with fury now. "But you know what you don't want to do? Tell the girl to get her ass back up when she says she's falling in love with you."

And she was yelling now. Drawing attention from tourists on the streets, but he couldn't really blame her.

She turned again and moved quickly back down the street, clearly familiar with the way back to the flat. He made no attempt to stop her now, knowing the best way to see this out was to simply talk at the flat. Though who the fook knew what he was even going to say.

By the time he reached the building, she was facing away from him waiting for him to unlock the door. Once he did she moved inside and up the stairs to their floor. The process was repeated until they reached the flat and had closed the door behind them.

"Can we talk now?"

"I think talking may be the problem." She gave a harsh laugh. "Evidently I should've just kept my mouth shut."

"You know I don't do relationships, Lana," he said tersely, a bit desperately. They shouldn't be in this situation. She'd known going in who he was. "For fook's sake, you're twenty-four. I figured shagging you was harmless. You shouldn't be searching for love right now, you should be havin' fun."

She flinched, and he saw some color leach from her face. But her fighting spirit didn't diminish a bit.

"Since you're so quick to generalize about me, hey, you're what, thirty-four? Why *aren't* you looking for love?"

He was thirty-five. His jaw clenched and he shook his head. "Love is hard. Lust is easy."

"Really. Is that the mantra you chant in your head all day

long?"

Aye, actually it was.

"And that's all this is. Lust?" she continued. "So then what was that whole *you're mine* business last night then? When you got so ridiculously possessive in bed?"

Christ. He'd hoped she'd forgotten that. Or maybe had been too swept up in passion to remember. Even though the memory of it had stayed in *his* head, disturbingly clear, all day.

"The alcohol from last night maybe," he muttered.

"No. *I* was the buzzed one—you were sober." She folded her arms across her chest and waited for him to reply.

"Look," he said carefully, "we all say things we don't mean in the heat of sex."

She didn't even flinch now. "So you didn't mean it. Any of it."

His heart stuttered as he tried to respond. His tongue grew thick in his mouth.

Tell her you didn't mean it.

"So you're saying, hypothetically—" she shrugged "—that you would be totally okay if I walked out of this flat and found some other guy to go home with tonight?"

No he sure as fook wouldn't be okay with that. Just imagining it made his blood pressure spike. And the realization it was spiking confused the hell out of him. He shouldn't be angry over that. He didn't want more than a casual fling. He never cared if a woman wanted to see someone else. But the idea of Delonna going off to find another bloke did *not* sit well.

"The truth, Aleck."

"The truth..." As if it were that simple. "The truth is... no. And I realize I'm an arse for saying it, but I wouldn't be okay with you finding some other bloke tonight. I'd be jealous." He paused. "And, aye, I realize I've no right to that jealousy."

"No right whatsoever," she agreed in a low trembling voice. She turned away and strode down the hallway of the flat.

"Lana..."

"I want to be alone. I'm going to take a bath and hopefully, when I get done, you'll have gone out somewhere."

He closed his eyes and his lips twisted into a bitter grimace. "If that's what you'd like, then I can leave you for a bit."

She didn't reply and a moment later the door closed behind her. The bathwater turned on and he knew this conversation was done.

How had things gone to such complete shite? How had he not realized she was getting attached?

Ah, fook everything.

He grabbed his coat and left the flat.

DELONNA SAT ON the edge of the toilet watching the

bathwater run, but making no attempt to get into the tub.

She heard the click of the apartment door opening and then closing a moment later. He'd left her, just as she'd basically ordered him to.

Tears burned her eyes and she scrubbed at them, hating herself for being brought to this state. And as much as she wanted to hate him, hate his reaction, she was angrier with herself.

He was right. She'd known he didn't do relationships. Had known exactly what she'd gotten herself into by going to bed with her player boss.

How was this even possible? Could she just be confused? She'd just gotten out of a long-term relationship. Granted, a shitty one that she'd never really felt anything but lust in. She could acknowledge that now.

Then there was Aleck. The boss and friend she'd been flirting with for years, and what, after finally sleeping with each other for a week or so, she was falling in love with him?

Maybe it wasn't love. Maybe it was the enchantment of Edinburgh. The hazy vacation filter that made everything more romantic. What she did know was Aleck was the first guy she'd ever said the "L" word to.

After stripping off her clothes, she climbed into the bath and tried to wash away the misery that cloaked her.

"Aleck? Really, Delonna," she whispered to herself. "You should've known better."

And the more she thought about it, the more she started

to realize that maybe she'd ambushed him with this love thing. It was too soon to put that kind of weight on someone.

Her unhappiness mingled now with embarrassment. She should've kept her mouth shut up there at the castle. Should've taken time to analyze the emotions in her heart before throwing them out there in what probably had felt like a verbal assault.

There was no denying he'd handled it horribly, but in a way, she couldn't blame him. Aleck didn't do permanent. Kenzie had warned her. She'd seen the evidence herself. And, what, she'd thought she'd change him? Stupid.

And now here they were stuck together for the rest of the week in a flat in Scotland.

Awkward times a billion…

~

WHEN SHE CAME out of the bathroom an hour later, the flat was quiet and it became clear that Aleck hadn't come back.

They needed to talk. To smooth over the mess she'd made of things this afternoon. If they were going to get through this week together, then she'd just tell him she'd been caught up in the moment.

A stab of guilt hit as she thought about Aleck's parents. They hadn't checked in with them since this morning. Maybe she should go stop by. And maybe, hopefully, Aleck was down there with them now.

She threw on a long sweater over leggings, slipped on flats and then left the apartment to go check on his parents.

After a quick knock on their door, it opened a moment later.

Brenda smiled, her face lighting up. "Hello, dear. You've not brought Aleck?"

So he wasn't here. Her heart sank. "No, um, he's out running around town. Probably needed a break from me."

There was far too much truth in that statement, which she'd meant to be a joke. But Brenda's eyes took on a knowing, almost weary look, and she gave a slow nod.

"Sometimes they do, luv. Come in." She stepped back and gestured for Delonna to come into the flat. "We could have some tea. Rodrick is taking a nap. Those pain pills can put him straight to sleep some days."

Soon they were sipping tea in the living room, chatting about harmless things, but fortunately no probing on whether Delonna and her son were in a relationship.

"Here, I've an album from when my kids were just wee things. A moment." Brenda disappeared and returned a moment later with the album, setting it on Delonna's lap.

Delonna flipped through it slowly, laughing and smiling at the pictures of the McLaughlin siblings as children. Kenzie's hair was bright and red, her eyes so green. Even at seven she was surrounded by boys in photos.

The twins, Ian and Colin, were always together in the pics and getting into all kinds of mischief. But Aleck was the most fascinating to her. So stoic in some of the photos, he always just seemed to be observing. Watching.

"Was he as serious of a kid as he looks in these pictures?" Delonna asked.

"He played hard and had his fun, but he was quite protective of his younger siblings and tended to watch for trouble rather than play often."

"He still is rather protective," she murmured, flipping the page and spotting a picture of Aleck in his element. "He played soccer?"

"It's referred to as football here, dear."

"Oh right."

Brenda grinned. "Took me a bit of getting used to as well."

Delonna glanced at the older woman. "Kenzie told me how you and your husband met while you were backpacking. It's very sweet. Do you prefer living in Scotland?"

Pursing her lips, Brenda seemed to give it a moment of speculation. "I love parts of both countries. Whidbey was gorgeous and quite a nice pace of life. But I fell in love with Scotland, even before I met Rodrick. I consider Edinburgh my true home—where my heart is—now."

"I can see why you would. What I saw today was gorgeous."

"I'm glad you find it lovely as well." Brenda gave her a considering look. "My son is quite taken with you."

Embarrassment stole through her and Delonna gave a

small shake of her head. Taken by lust maybe.

"You disagree?" his mother asked lightly.

How did you discuss this with the mother of the man you were sleeping with? You couldn't say you'd fallen in love with her son, but he didn't return the feelings. You couldn't even say that you were just screwing around.

"We have a complicated relationship," Delonna finally admitted carefully. "But the important thing is we're good friends."

"That is absolutely important. But I know my son." Understanding shone in the other woman's eyes now. "And if he has any sense left in him, he won't let you go."

Not quite sure what to say to that, Delonna just bit her lip and looked away.

"I apologize if that makes you a bit uncomfortable," Brenda added quietly. "I'm afraid I tend to say whatever is on me mind."

"You passed that trait on to at least a couple of your children, and I'm used to it." Delonna smiled and stood up. "Thank you for the tea, but I should probably get back to the flat in case Aleck is looking for me."

"Of course. Thank you for dropping by to check on us."

"I enjoyed our chat. Is there anything we can bring you tonight? Or how about breakfast tomorrow?"

"Come for breakfast. I'll prepare something for us all."

"Are you sure? We could bring something—"

"No need, I've plenty of food. But one moment, dear." Brenda disappeared down the hall and returned with a worn-looking shoebox. "These are just some of Aleck's old things, pictures and such, from years ago. Maybe you could help him sort through it and find what he really needs to hold on to, and what he doesn't?"

Now that seemed a bit of an odd request, but Delonna took the box and nodded. "I'll give it to him when he returns. See you in the morning, Brenda."

"Have a good night, dear."

Back in the flat upstairs, she realized Aleck still wasn't back. Her heart sank, and she wished they'd both set up their cell phones for international use. But they hadn't and she had no idea where he was. So she'd wait.

She set the shoebox on the kitchen table and stared down at it. Curiosity got the better of her, and she lifted the lid off, expecting to find a box full of pictures.

Brenda must've given her the wrong box, was Delonna's first reaction. There were some pictures, yes, but more so there were items. Weird, eclectic, not really masculine things.

A charm bracelet. Handwritten notes that had lipstick marks on them. She found a picture in a frayed paper-type frame and pulled it from the box. Some sort of school dance photo with a guy and a girl.

It was Aleck as a teenager, and he had some epically bad hair. The girl in his arms was a pretty brunette with big blue eyes. This must've been the teenage romance Kenzie had mentioned.

The door to the flat clicked open and she jumped back guiltily from the box.

Aleck stepped inside, his wary gaze seeking her out. "I tried to give you some time," he said cautiously. "I know it might not—What's this?"

She followed his gaze to the box and the guilt inside her multiplied.

"Your mom gave it to me to give to you. I shouldn't have opened it, but she suggested I help you go through it. I know it's none of my business." She was rambling. "I'm sorry."

He came closer and stared down at it. His face seemed to lose some color and his mouth tightened.

"I swore I'd thrown this box away." He reached out to touch the school dance picture that now sat on top. "Me ma must've found it and retrieved it from the garbage."

Delonna frowned, glancing back at the box. She started putting together the puzzle pieces in her head.

"Was she your girlfriend before you moved to America?"

"Aye." He smoothed his thumb over her face in the picture.

"You loved her, but it didn't end well?" she guessed. "You guys had some big fight and broke up, and then you moved to another country with your family?"

"You're right on most accounts, save for one part." His lips twisted into a bitter smile. "We didn't have a fight and break up."

"You didn't?"

"No. We'd probably be married right now..." He paused. "That is if Cassie hadn't gotten herself killed."

Chapter Sixteen

ALECK FELT A bit guilty for announcing it so bluntly when Delonna blanched and looked as if she might be sick.

"She's dead?"

"Aye, she was only seventeen," he said as he rummaged through the box. "I gave her this bracelet on her sixteenth birthday." He touched the daisy charm and smiled faintly. "She loved daisies."

Delonna was silent for a moment. "How did she die, if I may ask?"

"She was walking to the market when a drunk driver jumped the curb and hit her." He said it feeling almost matter-of-fact about it now. The years had severed most of the pain.

"Oh my God…"

"Before the accident, I had no intention of leaving with my family to America. I loved Cassie, and in another year I would've turned eighteen." He sighed. "We had made plans to marry."

"To marry..." she repeated faintly.

He dug around in the box and pulled out a slippery piece of paper, unfolding it from the square shape it had been folded into.

"She was pregnant." He touched the ultrasound picture, tracing the tiny baby with his finger. "She was not yet twelve weeks into the pregnancy when she was hit by the cabbie. She didn't die right away, but suffered a traumatic brain injury—was brain dead, you see. She, along with our baby, passed away within a few days."

When he glanced up, Delonna's expression was a mix of horror and stunned disbelief.

"Aleck. Oh my God, I don't even know what to say. Did your family know she was pregnant?"

"Only our parents, and they learned after the accident." He shook his head. "There was nothing to be done for the baby, though. It was too late. My siblings never knew about the baby, and I hope they never learn. It's quite a bit to take in, as you're realizing."

"Yes." Tears brimmed her eyes now.

"I wouldn't have laid it upon you either, Lana, but it seems my mother took that choice out of my hands." He gave a bitter smile.

Why had his ma given Delonna the box? Clearly she'd known what was in it.

Realization sank in. He knew his mother well enough to understand that maybe she'd been trying to help. To help

Delonna see why he was the way he was. Delonna had likely shown up at their flat earlier, and had probably still been in distress.

"I shouldn't have opened the box," she whispered. "This was your story to tell me and even then only if you wanted to."

"Actually, when I came back to the flat tonight, it was with the intention of telling you about Cassie." He set the ultrasound picture back in the box. "This is just a quick, more in-depth way of explaining, I suppose."

"And painful."

"Aye." He didn't deny it as he set the lid back on the shoebox. "Though much less painful now than it was back then. It felt as if me heart had damn near been ripped from me chest when I lost her." He turned and walked to the kitchen to pour a glass of water. "So in the end I went to America and buried the past—quite literally."

Delonna was silent and when he returned with a glass of water, he found her wiping a tear off her cheek.

"Can you maybe understand now why I fear you loving me?" he asked, searching her face. "Can you see why I can't love like that again?"

She nodded, dropping her gaze. "I understand. Really, I do."

Maybe she did, or maybe this topic was just so horrifying that she'd say anything to end it. He took a sip of water, letting the cold liquid slide down his throat. Focusing on that for just a moment.

"You'll never love anyone the way you loved her," Delonna said, almost inaudibly.

No, he realized, she didn't really understand. But maybe it was better that way.

"I'm sorry, Lana," he said softly. "For letting you find out like this, and for this afternoon. I was a complete bastart to you up at the castle," he admitted. "And I hope you can forgive me."

"I do. But only if you can do the same." She gave a poor attempt at a smile. "I shouldn't have dumped that announcement on you like that. I think...maybe I'm just confused by everything. The romance of Scotland. Good sex. All that adds up, right?"

Did it? Or was she just trying to make things easier on him?

He gave a faint smile. "So where do we go from here?"

She took his hand and gave it a gentle squeeze. "Where do you want to go?"

Where did he want to go? Straight to the bedroom. And maybe that made him a bit fooked up after they'd been discussing his dead girlfriend from his teenage years. Here was this woman in front of him who was vibrant with life, and who'd somehow made him start to care about someone who wasn't considered family. It went beyond lust—he knew it, even if he refused to let it be love.

"I see," she said softly. "Come on."

Did she see, he wondered? But realized she did when she led him down the hall to their room and undressed him slowly and deliberately, then did the same to herself.

He did very little, too emotionally drained now, but his body awake with the need to have her. She seemed to know that and took control, easing him onto his back on the bed.

She was gentle with him. Touching and tasting him nearly everywhere, before taking his erection with her mouth and bringing him near to the edge.

"Lana," he groaned her name softly, holding her hair. Closing himself off from the past and focusing only on the present and the pleasure Delonna was giving him.

When she pulled back it was only to move on top of him a moment later. To take complete control of the lovemaking and ride them both into pleasure.

When it was over and she was curled into his arms, he closed his eyes and waited for his heart to slow to normal. He pressed a kiss to her forehead, feeling strangely vulnerable and so damn grateful.

"Thank you."

"You're welcome, boss boy." Her reply was almost a whisper, before she rested her head on his chest.

There was no other way to describe what had just happened other than complete and tender lovemaking. And as much as Delonna wanted to convince him her declaration at the castle had been bogus, he knew every touch just now had been an act of love. Knew by the way she gave herself to him so completely and intimately. The way she folded herself into his arms right now.

It simultaneously petrified him and sparked something inside his heart that had seemed dead to other lovers. He knew every day he spent with Delonna made him more in danger of falling for her—if he hadn't already. He already knew her better than he had any lover since Cassie.

His blood pounded harder and a feeling of dread built in his belly. Love someone the way he had Cassie? He couldn't do it. He couldn't go through that kind of pain again. It didn't matter that it had been nearly twenty years; he could remember the pain of losing her as if it were yesterday.

He'd sworn to never care about someone that much again. Had done a damn good job at keeping the women in his life fleeting. Enough to satisfy the itch to be intimate with someone, but never long enough to fall in love.

And it really hadn't been that long with Delonna, but apparently he hadn't needed that long for something to click into place between them.

"I promised your mother we'd be there for breakfast."

She was rather good with his parents. She was rather good at many things.

"Starbucks again?"

"No, she wants to cook."

"You're in a for a treat. Eggs. Tomatoes. Beans. Bacon—quite different, bacon from ours though, just to warn you."

"I'm not picky about my meat."

Another brilliant thing about her, it seemed. Why the fook couldn't he let the past go? Move on and give them a chance?

She unfurled from his arms and climbed out of bed. "It's too early to sleep. Want to find something to watch on TV?"

"Aye." A bit of mindless distraction sounded perfect, actually. He slid out of bed and followed after her.

"HOW WAS BREAKFAST?"

"Wonderful. And filling."

Aleck watched as Delonna leaned back in her chair and pressed a hand to her stomach. She'd nearly cleaned her plate, which was pretty common for anyone eating his mother's cooking.

"Good to hear. We've a surprise for you." His mother stood up and left the kitchen, returning a moment later with a set of keys.

"What's this?" Aleck asked when she made to give them to him.

"The car is full of petrol and you're to take Delonna for a drive into the Highlands."

Aleck frowned, casting his father an uncertain look.

"We'll not take no for an answer, Son," his da agreed. "We'll manage a day alone just fine. Have done so up 'til you arrived anyway."

"But we came to spend time with you and assist in Rodrick's recovery," Delonna said hesitantly. "I don't need to make this into a sightseeing trip."

"Nonsense. You've been helping out plenty." His ma brushed aside her protests. "This is your first trip to Scotland, and who knows when you'll get back. You must see a few things, dear."

"We'll not take no for an answer," his da repeated. "Tomorrow I've an appointment you can drive me to, but there's nothing we need today."

"Right then." Aleck grimaced and accepted the keys. "We'll be back by nightfall to check on you."

Rodrick eased from his chair at the table, looking stronger today than he had yesterday even. He waved away any attempts Aleck or Delonna made to assist him.

"No need to rush, Son, we'll be just fine," his da called out as he made his way down the hall. "Though if you could help me grab a towel from the closet here?"

"I'll help." Delonna was on her feet and down the hall in a moment. It gave Aleck the time alone with his mother that he'd hoped for.

"You gave Delonna my box."

His mother didn't even pretend to not understand and lifted her chin to meet his stare unwavering. "She had a right to know the ghosts she was up against if she's going to love my son."

He flinched and shook his head. "I would've told her."

"Aye? Well, I couldn't be certain." His mother leaned

forward. "It's long past the time you let Cassie go, Aleck. Time to let yourself love again. You're not getting any younger, and surely you want a wife. A family."

"He's settling in to take a shower." Delonna returned from the hallway. "Refused any help other than handing him the towel."

"Sounds about right." His mother smiled. "Thank you for all your help, Delonna. You're an incredible woman."

"Oh. Thank you." Delonna's eyes had widened. "That's, um, very sweet of you to say."

He knew what his mother was doing and he wasn't going to bite. "Thank you for the car and the suggested day in the Highlands." He kissed her cheek. "We'll be sure to have fun."

"Oh, one last thing, Aleck," his mother said quickly. "I almost forgot to tell you that your brother Colin called and asked that I give you a message."

"Oh aye?"

"He said you'd be very interested to hear that someone named James has been located and arrested?"

Chapter Seventeen

"I CAN'T BELIEVE they found him," Delonna murmured as they sat in morning traffic to get out of Edinburgh.

Aleck snorted. "I can. The wanker was stupid enough to send you a text message. I don't care if it wasn't from his phone, I'm sure with a little detective work he wasn't all that hard to trace."

"I'm so relieved. But what if…what if that other guy who has been harassing me doesn't back off?"

"Then I'll hunt him down and shove his bollocks down his throat. Simple as that, luv."

She laughed, but her heart wasn't really in it. *Love*. It had never bothered her when he'd used the endearment before, but now, when he was clearly so against falling in love with her, it stung a little.

"This traffic is just as bad as Seattle's," she said, to change the subject. "Which is why I live on Whidbey now."

"It's much lighter on Whidbey," he agreed.

The traffic began to ease up moments later and soon they were out of the city and moving almost briskly on the road.

"You should stay with me still."

She glanced at him, frowning. "Stay with you?"

"Back on Whidbey. Since you're worried about the guy who's been harassing you."

"Oh." She'd forgotten all about returning to the island and then actually going home to her rental she shared with Kenzie. Leaving Aleck's place. It left her a bit hollow. "I'm sure I'll be fine now."

He didn't answer, and a good amount of the drive into the Highlands was spent in silence. Part of it was her trying not to cry, and part of her was just being so blown away by the beauty of the land around them.

There were mountains and hills, some in brilliant shades of green, while some were more of a brownish yellow. Now and then some were snowcapped. The mountains held gentle curves, though some were more dramatic and sharp in their points. In one spot a deep dramatic valley ran between the hills and they parked to get out to look around and take pictures.

"They filmed a Bond movie here," Aleck said.

"James Bond?"

"Aye."

"I can see why. Here. Let's get a pic." She forced Aleck to do a selfie with her. It was the only pic she'd have of them together, and when it was taken and she stared at it, she could only smile as she noted how stoic he looked in the picture. He was the same as the child from years ago.

"Gorgeous," she said, turning back to the view and stuffing her phone into the pocket of her jeans. "It literally takes my breath away. It's so vast. So stark. I can't believe people lived in these hills."

"Me neither. Not nearly close enough to a Starbucks for me taste. Come, let's get back in the car and drive to a nearby town to have lunch."

Lunch was at a tiny town that really had just a restaurant and a store attached. It was cozy and completely unique, and after a small simple lunch, Aleck walked her over to a nearby pasture where a peculiar-looking animal was grazing.

"What is that?" Delonna asked, leaning against the fence. "Some type of bull?"

"What you're looking at, luv, is a Highland cow."

"A Highland cow," she repeated and then something pricked in the back of her mind.

"Didn't you once say I was more attractive than a Highland cow?"

Aleck squinted his gaze at the cow. "Mmm. I'm not quite sure I remember—"

"No, you really did. And if this hairy, red thing, obviously lacking a few brain cells is a Highland cow, then I should probably be a little insulted," she teased.

"Well, if you must. But be warned, you'll have hurt its feelings." He smiled and cast her a sideways glance. "It's different taking you here. Someone new to Scotland. My siblings and I come at least once every year or two."

"I would too if I were in your shoes. Family would be the excuse to get me here. The scenery and charm would make me stay as long as I could." She hesitated. "Would you ever move back?"

He didn't answer right away. "I love Whidbey quite a bit, but I'll never say never."

She nodded, suspecting that some day he would indeed come back. Follow in his parents' footsteps. But he would come back alone, without a wife.

Her heart did that little twisty and achy thing that was becoming all too familiar the last couple of days. The unhappiness that she'd managed to smother with the sights of Scotland was never deep enough buried. She'd had to come to terms with the truth.

Aleck moved to rub her back, the gesture comforting and without sexual intent. A few days ago it wouldn't have bothered her in the least. Today, it was like rubbing salt in a wound.

She stared at the cow, focusing on the awkward and yet fascinating beast, and knowing what she had to do.

"Aleck?"

"Mmm?"

"I need to stop sleeping with you."

The hand on her back stilled and the air between them was suddenly heavy with unspoken words. She couldn't say more. Didn't even need to, because clearly he had to know why she'd said it.

Finally: "I understand."

He accepted it so easily that her heart split a little more and tears pricked at the back of her eyes. Yesterday when they'd made love she'd wanted it to be all for him. Bringing him pleasure. Bringing him peace and comfort with her touch. And in the process she'd lost a little bit of herself again, even as she knew it had been healing for Aleck.

They had four more days here in Scotland, and she'd be spending it out of his arms. Out of his bed. If she were going to survive without giving him another little piece of her heart, she had to nip this in the bud now.

"We can be—" she swallowed hard "—just friends again. Okay?"

"Aye. Friends is good," he said quietly.

BETWEEN SEEING MORE sights and helping out with his dad, the days passed quickly. It was the nights that seemed to drag on. Aleck had spent the rest of them on the couch, while she'd slept in the big bed. Used to sleeping alone, she'd gotten all too accustomed to being with Aleck. It was lonely, cold and depressing. She hadn't had a good sleep since they'd slipped back into friend mode.

The morning they were scheduled to fly home, they said their goodbyes at the airport to Aleck's mom. Rodrick had stayed home to rest, having said his farewells earlier.

"It was lovely to spend the week with you, Delonna."

Brenda kissed her cheek and stared down at her. "I hope you enjoyed your trip."

"Of course I did. It was such a pleasure getting to know you."

Aleck's mom gave a slight smile, but her eyes were troubled. Delonna knew she had sensed things had taken a turn for the worse between her and Aleck.

"I'm sorry," the older woman whispered, barely audible as she glanced at her son who was moving the luggage toward the airport doors. "I had hoped…"

Delonna hugged the other woman again and shook her head. "It's fine." *It isn't.* "I knew going in what to expect." *I just completely ignored it.*

"All right, Ma." Aleck returned and pulled his mother into a big hug. "Good to see you as always. Don't let Da be such a grump, and keep him active, aye?"

"Always do. Love you, Son." She looked as if she wanted to say more, but Aleck kissed her cheek and then turned Delonna's way.

"Ready?"

Delonna nodded against the lump in her throat. Time to go back to real life.

~

GETTING BACK TO normal was bloody awful. Not just because of the adjustment to the time change, but because Aleck was once again alone.

And with no one but yourself to blame, he reminded himself as he made his way through the pub, checking up on things.

"You look exhausted—go home." Kenzie appeared in the doorway to his office several minutes later, her forehead wrinkled into a frown.

"I'll head back in a bit," he muttered.

"Have you even slept since returning?"

"A few hours each night, but my body is still all out of sorts from the time change."

Kenzie shut the door to the office and leaned against it. "What happened between you and Delonna? She's moved back into the rental—which is a really bad sign after you've just spent the week together in Scotland."

"There's no reason for her not to move back. The threat is gone, and… You know, it's none of your fookin' business really. It was just time for her to go home." He almost made it sound like he'd kicked her out, when she was the one to leave.

"You totally blew it with her, didn't you?"

Completely. But it was safer to his sanity this way. His heart.

"Again, none of your business." He moved from his desk to kiss his sister's cheek. "But thanks again for taking care of things while I was gone. Things went well?"

"Perfectly." She didn't look happy with the subject change, but went along with it. "The window was replaced and I think the excitement of being shot up actually brought in more customers."

He grimaced. "Good to hear humanity's thirst for violence is strong as ever."

"You know James made bail."

Aleck stilled. "He'll be convicted when it goes to trial. Has he made any attempt to see her?"

"No." Kenzie hesitated. "But he's out there and could at any point."

"Have there been any threats against her from that other guy?"

"No. As far as I can see, she's safe." Kenzie sighed. "But she's not happy. She hasn't left her room. I can hear her crying at times."

Aleck's chest tightened almost painfully.

"And she'd kill me if she found out I'd told you that. But I just knew you'd end up hurting her," Kenzie continued quietly. "I warned her. I just, dammit, Aleck, it's Delonna. Could you not have just left her alone in the first place?"

"I wanted to," he rasped, thrusting a hand through his hair. His heart thumped quicker in his chest. "Fook, I tried. I really did. I just... I couldn't."

There was a heavy silence and when he finally got control of his emotions and glanced at his sister, she stared at him with dawning comprehension.

"Holy shit on a stick." Her eyes were wide and her brows drawn together. "I almost don't believe it, but I think you're in love with her."

"No."

"Aye. Like it or not, Brother, it's happened."

"The fook it has," he snapped, striding past her to grab and drink a bit of the pint he'd poured himself earlier.

Kenzie followed him. "It's quite amazing how you can have so much advice, so much insight on your siblings' love lives. Be so spot on sometimes, and yet be utterly blind when it comes to your own heart."

He closed his eyes and tried to block out the wash of despondency that moved through him.

"You don't understand." He shook his head, his voice cracking. "I can't go through that again. I can't love someone that much."

"I know how much you loved Cassie. How much she meant to you." Kenzie touched his shoulder. "Maybe you never told any of us, but even as young as I was, I could see it. And I saw the change in you after it happened."

He stared at his little sister, a bit amazed at how much she'd been able to surmise back then.

"Is it that you don't think you can ever love someone that much again?" Kenzie asked, seeming genuinely confused.

"It's not that I can't love. Clearly I can. Some people you love by default, like family. But I've no desire to ever romantically love a woman that deeply again. So much that it nearly destroys you when something happens to them."

"But that's a risk we all take. It's a risk I take every time Brett gets sent out on the boat." Kenzie looked dismayed. "Do you really want to just grow old alone?"

"Aye, that's the plan."

"And you don't want children?"

"I'll have me nieces and nephews to keep me busy. You and Brett should start right on that," he tried to tease.

She didn't take the bait. "You don't ever want a wife? A partner in life?"

"No wife," he agreed, feeling strangely empty now.

"Then there's no hope for you." Unhappiness and disbelief shone on his sister's face. "If I thought you could make it work with anyone, it would've been Delonna."

"I've been clear to everyone what my intentions are in life." Fook, why the hell wouldn't she drop it already? His head began to throb.

Kenzie didn't back down, but went toe to toe with him. "Tell me, to my face, that you don't love her."

"Dammit all to hell. I don't love her, Kenzie," he yelled, smashing the pint glass against the wall. "Do you hear me? I don't love her and I'll *never* love her. Is that clear enough for you?"

"It's clear enough for me."

It wasn't Kenzie who answered, but Delonna. He hadn't heard the door to the office open. Hadn't seen her come in.

Her eyes were bloodshot and strangely devoid of emotion. She wore no makeup and appeared as if she'd been in the same sweatpants and hoodie for days.

Shame slammed through him hard, making him start to almost shake as bile rose in his throat.

"Ah shite." He stepped forward. "Delonna—"

"It looks like I've made the right choice." She stepped past Kenzie and held out a piece of paper to him.

He didn't take it. "What's this?"

"I'm quitting. I'm old-fashioned and put it on paper." Her mouth almost twitched with a semblance of a smile.

Kenzie shot him the most vile, loathing look ever, but he couldn't acknowledge it as he stared at Delonna.

"You don't want to do this." His words were unsteady as he reached for her.

She sidestepped him, dropping the paper on the floor as he refused to take it. "I do want to do this. I have to do this. I'm sure you'd rather not lose your moneymaker of a bartender, but you'll find someone to replace me. Both at the pub and in your bed."

That was a low blow.

"Aleck," Kenzie hissed, clearly telling him to fix this.

"Don't leave. I fooked up, Lana." He caught her wrist as she tried to move away.

"No you didn't, I did. I slept with and fell in love with my boss. I knew the risks involved, and I knew you didn't want serious." She met his gaze now, solidly and without judgment in her eyes. She tugged her wrist free and backed away from him.

"We can work through this..."

"I can't compete with someone who's dead. I said I loved you up on the castle and nothing's changed. But since you can't accept that love, and you clearly can't return it..." She gave a helpless shrug. "I'm out, Aleck."

"Lana," he choked out, stepping after her.

"No." She shook her head, turned on her heel and walked out of his office.

"Well congratulations," Kenzie said, her voice low and shaking. "You've just let the best thing that ever happened to you walk out of your life."

~

SHE COULD ALWAYS turn to ice cream, but right now ice cream wasn't really the patch for the hole in her heart. Delonna closed the freezer and then went to grab a tissue to blow her nose again.

Fortunately Kenzie was at work and didn't have to bear witness to this ridiculous meltdown. Though she'd been there to witness the end of her and Aleck at the pub an hour ago, but Delonna had been so focused on just getting through that moment she'd barely noticed her friend standing nearby.

And now here she was with no job, no guy and no damn idea what her future looked like. Even though James had been arrested, the police had only recovered one thousand dollars of her stolen money.

Maybe she'd go look through the online ads of who was hiring. Though she knew she wouldn't have much trouble getting another bartending job. On more than one occasion the owner of another bar had approached her. He'd made it clear she could have a job if she were ever interested.

The sound of someone unlocking her door had her glancing toward it, hope flaring in her heart that maybe, just maybe, Aleck had pulled his head out of his ass.

But when it swung open a moment later, she realized again how stupid she'd been. Both to hope Aleck would have a change of heart, and to have not bolted the door.

"You just broke into my house," she said in disbelief as James stepped through the door and closed it behind him.

"Is it really breaking in if you gave me a key at one point?" He frowned. "Ah, you're still crying over me? That's kind of sweet. And weird."

"I'm not crying over *you*, and haven't you fucking done enough?" Vibrating with anger, she strode toward him and used all her strength to slap him in the face. "That's for stealing my money, asshole. And ouch."

She gripped her wrist and winced. Despite the look of surprise on his face, James didn't look too put out. She'd never feared he'd hurt her, not now and not when they'd dated. He wasn't the violent sort, just more of a jerk.

"Like I said, I didn't really have any choice. I'm in a world of trouble, babe."

"You sure are." She went in search of her purse to find

her phone to call 911. Maybe him showing up here was violating the terms of his bail. She'd sure try and find out.

James grabbed her purse from her hand before she could reach her phone. "If you're going for your phone, I can't let you do that."

"Are you just really stupid or what?" she demanded.

"He's after me. That bookie is after me."

"Oh? Well then good. I'm glad his focus has moved from me to you."

"He's going to kill me, D. Don't you care? I don't have his money and he knows it. I spent most of your money just getting out of town."

"And now you're back because your stupid ass sent me a text and got traced and arrested. Sorry if I have no sympathy for you." She reached for her purse but he held it over her head. "Give that back!"

"I need money."

"You took all my money, and even if I had some, I sure as hell wouldn't give it to you." Her emotions were on overload from this morning with Aleck, and now this. "God, just *get out.*"

"Babe—"

"Don't call me babe. Don't call me anything. Just get the hell out." She kicked at his knees and he jumped back with a laugh.

"Whoa, getting a little violent, D."

"Get out, I said!" She grabbed a lamp, ready to swing it

at his head.

"Whoa, whoa, whoa. Easy. Okay." He dropped her purse and backed slowly toward the door. "Fine, I'll go."

"I hope you get life in prison!" It was a childish and completely inane statement, because even some murderers didn't get life in prison. And this shithead had just stolen six grand from her.

"Can't wait to see you at trial, babe."

He was going to skip town. She saw it in his eyes. *Motherfucker.*

A moment later he was gone and out the door, and she didn't have the energy to go after him. She went to grab her phone and debated calling the police, but then set it down again. What was the point? Right now she didn't have the energy for anything.

Maybe ice cream and some shitty reality TV. Yeah. That sounded like a pretty good idea.

Encouraged with her new plan, she went to the freezer and grabbed the container. She pried the lid off, ready to devour the rest of the chocolate mint deliciousness and then froze.

"Son of a *bitch*."

As if her day wasn't shitty enough, she was completely out of ice cream.

~

ALECK WAS JUST getting ready to leave work when his

brother walked into the back room at the pub.

Colin looked quite somber, and Aleck bit back a sigh, thinking news must've traveled fast from Kenzie.

"I don't want to hear it," Aleck muttered, lifting his hand. "I've heard enough from Kenzie as it is. I know I've hurt her, and I feel like a bloody bastart, but there's nothing to be done—"

"There's been an accident."

Chapter Eighteen

ALECK BLINKED, HIS heart quickening and his palms going damp. Those words were eerily similar to what he'd heard nearly twenty years ago.

"An accident?" he repeated, his words low and unsteady. "Delonna?"

"Aye."

Aleck came around the desk, his heart going a mile a minute now. "What kind of accident. Is she all right?"

Colin didn't answer right away, and the sick feeling of dread in Aleck's chest exploded.

"Where is she? What happened?" he asked thickly, reaching for his keys.

"A call came in from a concerned citizen, reporting a vehicle speeding dangerously," Colin said, his voice low and unsteady. "They were able to give a license plate right before the witness saw the car go off a cliff into the Sound."

"No. *No.*" He knew where this was leading.

"Aleck…it was Delonna's car. I'm so sorry. They haven't recovered the vehicle yet, but are working on it. But with the time that's passed since it sank..." Colin paused, pain and regret flashing in his eyes "...they're now calling it a recovery, not a rescue mission."

"I don't believe it." Aleck was going to be sick. He staggered around through the office toward the bathroom, but standing over the toilet, nothing came out.

Colin appeared in the doorway. "I'm so fuckin' sorry, Aleck."

Closing his eyes, Aleck let the denial rock through him. The rage and pain hit with the force of a tsunami.

No. *Jesus Christ no.*

He grabbed his keys. "Where," he choked out. "Where is she?"

Colin gave him the location and rushed on. "You're in no condition to drive, Aleck. Please, just stay here. Ian and Sarah are bringing the baby and coming over."

Aleck pushed past him, keys in hand, and ran out the door. He was half blind from the tears in his eyes as he climbed into his car.

He knew exactly where the accident was said to have happened, but his mind and heart wouldn't let him believe it as he drove to the scene.

"Please God," he whispered. "Don't let this be true. It can't happen twice. It can't."

When he arrived on the location though, he was met with a mass of emergency responders and curious onlookers. He pushed his way through the crowd, trying to reach the edge of the cliff where the car had gone off the road.

He reached it just in time to see her car being slowly pulled from the water. Could see the shape of a body up front.

Grief ripped through him and he barely made it back to his car before falling to his knees with a sob. How was this happening? How the fook was this happening? Delonna was dead. He'd lost her. Just as he'd lost Cassie. Only this time, the pain was tenfold.

He climbed into the car and behind the wheel. This was all his fault. He may as well have driven that car off the cliff himself. Did she do it intentionally?

Not even realizing where he was going, he found himself driving toward her and Kenzie's house. His sister had left work earlier, and maybe she would have answers. Give some light on what had happened.

She's dead, that's what happened.

He had to pull over when he was sure he was going to be sick. He opened the door, felt the bile in his throat, but all he could do was dry heave. His eyes burned as if rubbed with sandpaper. He closed the door and started driving again.

When he pulled up outside Kenzie's house, he hoped like hell he'd see Delonna's car out front. Somehow convinced himself he would. That maybe this was just some big mistake. Maybe it was a car that was the same make and model as hers.

And the same license plate?

He stumbled out of the car and went to the front door. He didn't bother knocking, and realized it was unlocked anyway. He stumbled inside.

"Kenzie," he cried out hoarsely, moving blindly down the hall. "Oh God. *Kenzie*! She's dead. She's fookin' *dead*."

There were soft footsteps, then: "Who's dead?"

~

WHEN ALECK TURNED around to face her in the hallway, Delonna swore he went about four shades paler.

"You're alive," he whispered, eyes round and pupils dilated with shock.

"I guess that's debatable. I mean, technically, yes. I have a pulse. Emotionally, I'm a little dead."

He stared at her as if he'd seen a ghost, then moved toward her, touching her cheek with trembling fingers. Smoothing away the moisture there.

"Tears." The word was full of wonder. "You're really here?"

"Yes, I'm really here. Aleck, what kind of question is that?" She pulled away, and brushed away the moisture still gathered in her eyes. "And I'm crying because one, you're an asshole. And two, I'm out of ice cream—I had to resort to yogurt. I fucking hate yogurt…" She trailed off. "Wait, why are *you* crying?"

"Because I thought you were dead," he rasped. "Your car went over a cliff into the Sound."

"My car? I've been home all night. It must be someone else. My car is right out front."

"No, it's not."

Delonna dropped her spoon back into the yogurt, set it down on the table in the living room and then rushed to her purse, digging through it.

"My keys are gone. After all that son of a bitch did to me, he stole my car too? Seriously?"

She turned around, ready to run outside and check to see if her car was indeed gone, but smacked into Aleck.

He had her in his arms before she could blink, pulled so tight she could scarcely breathe.

"Aleck," she gasped.

"Please, just let me hold you for a moment." He pressed her cheek into his shoulder as his hands moved over her back.

So confused, she tried to put the pieces together. He'd thought she was dead. James had stolen her car. Had gone over a cliff?

"Wait. James is dead?" she whispered unevenly.

"If he was the one driving your car, then aye. Someone was killed in that vehicle. I watched it being pulled from the water. Colin was the one to tell me you'd been killed."

It sank in and her stomach twisted. The hair on the back of her neck lifted. "So there're a bunch of people who think I'm dead right now? We need to let them know I'm okay, Aleck. Now."

"Aye. Of course." He pulled away, visibly struggling to compose himself. "Let me call Colin."

She waited while he made the call, heard their low and emotional exchange. When Aleck slid his phone away a moment later, he turned immediately back to her.

"Colin is letting everyone know you're all right," Aleck said unsteadily. His gaze unwavering on her. "He said they think the brake lines in your car were cut. If James hadn't stolen your car, it could've very well been you. He said they've got a pretty good idea who this bookie is, and are sending in a team to get him tonight."

She could've been dead. Her brake lines were cut. That was enough to make her start to shake.

"Also, the police will be over in an hour to question you. Not a minute sooner."

"An hour?"

"I need at least an hour, luv."

"An hour for what?" She gave a small shrug.

He closed the distance between them and lifted her off the ground in two seconds flat.

"Aleck!"

He ignored her panicked cry, carrying her straight back to the bedroom and depositing her on the bed.

"What the—"

He was on top of her in an instant, his mouth covering hers in a frenzied, desperate kiss. When his mouth left hers to travel down her neck she shook her head.

"Aleck," she pleaded weakly. "We can't do this anymore."

He ignored her, pushing her shirt up over her breasts and making a groan of pleasure when he found them braless.

His lips closed around her nipple a moment later and she lost all ability to protest. His hands and mouth were everything. Touching her and tasting her. His gaze, every time it moved over her, a confusing mix of agony and relief.

When he thrust into her moments later, their fingers were laced, and she gave herself completely to him. Tears were in her eyes at knowing she was falling right back down that rabbit hole of love. Who was she kidding? She'd never gotten out.

Soon they were both boneless and spent, bodies intertwined and hearts pounding in near unison. But nothing had really changed, she thought. Maybe this was one last, relief-filled lovemaking celebrating the fact she was alive, but it couldn't happen again. She wasn't strong enough to survive it again.

She tried to pull away from him, feeling tears roll down her cheeks, but he held firm in his grip around her waist.

"I love you," he whispered. "I didn't want to love you, but in the end I couldn't stop it any more than I could stop the setting sun."

She closed her eyes and her heart twisted. "You're only saying this because you thought I'd died, Aleck."

"Aye, maybe that's what finally *made* me say it. But I felt it long before I admitted the truth. I knew I loved you in Edinburgh." He gave an incredulous laugh. "But I denied it to you, and to myself. Because I refused to go through the pain of losing someone again. And then...for nearly an hour, I thought I had."

She stroked his cheek, touched and amazed to find a tear on it. Just like the tear on her own.

"And denying I loved you didn't make it hurt any less in the end," he continued raggedly. "It hurt more, Lana, because I thought you'd died without knowing the truth. That I loved you. That I loved you so fookin' much I didn't even know who I was without you anymore."

Tears spilled down her cheeks and she shook her head. "I think I knew, Aleck. That you were just afraid to love again. But I thought you'd never open up. You'd never give us a chance."

"I want more than a chance." He flipped her onto her back and climbed on top of her again, his gaze holding hers. "I want everything, Lana. I want marriage, I want babies, and I want everything I'm so terrified of losing again. I want to take that chance that life will turn out okay. That we'll have forever."

"It will turn out okay," she promised, her heart so full now.

"And, if you'll have it, I want you to take not just my name, but half of McLaughlin's Pub. Be a co-owner, luv. There's no need to start your own."

Her breath caught and her eyes rounded. "That's huge. Are you sure?"

"I've never been more certain about anything in my life," he said thickly. "And I know you're young, and if you want to wait on marriage and children, I'll wait until you're ready."

"I don't need to wait." She gave a choked laugh. "I've waited this long for you to come to your senses. I love you so much, if there were a minister in the room I'd marry you now."

She felt his body stir to life again, and a moment later he began to ease back inside her.

"You'd get married now? While we're doing this?"

Pleasure shone in her eyes. "Why not?"

"He might be scandalized."

"I don't mind a good scandal." She closed her eyes as passion took over. "*Aleck.*"

"*Lana.*"

For once she let herself think beyond the passionate moment, knew that this was so much more than just sex and lust. This was the man she loved. Her future. The father of her future children.

"I love you," she whispered.

"I love you more."

"The fook you do."

"Mmm. The fook I do." He sank deep. "And veery well."

"Aye, you do." She smiled and pulled his head down for

another kiss.

~

NEVER WOULD SHE have thought it possible to be this happy. Brenda McLaughlin looked around the family barbeque and felt her heart swell with emotion.

Happiness had been a constant in her life since she'd met Rodrick and they'd made their own challenging way to a happily ever after.

But now, her happiness expanded further than her four children and amazing husband. They were still her children, but now they were all grown up and blissfully married with kids.

There were grandchildren, one old enough to be texting her boyfriend on her cell phone, another at the age where he could run from his grandpa as Rodrick chased him about the backyard, and then a bunch of chubby-faced babies. This, being a grandmother, was Brenda's heaven on earth.

"Can I get you another glass of wine?"

She smiled as her son-in-law approached. "That would be lovely, thank you, Brett."

When he returned a moment later with her glass, she accepted it with a murmur of thanks. He stayed by her side, lingering on the porch and staring out over the backyard as she did the same.

"Y'all should be proud of them. You raised amazing kids."

"I am proud. And I must say, you all are doing a lovely job raising my equally amazing grandchildren."

Pride swept across Brett's face. "Thank you. I think we're doing all right. And it seems like your kids learned from the best, with you and Rodrick. You're a good solid couple."

"We've had our highs and lows. Every couple does. But love, love and a determination to keep the love alive is what will keep two people together."

"Yes, ma'am. I couldn't agree more."

She glanced first at Kenzie, who was carrying an infant on her chest, while chasing down their two-year-old, and then glanced at Delonna and Aleck who each held one of the newborn twins.

"Brett, a little help over here?" Kenzie cried, clearly needing assistance with their preschooler.

He grinned and dashed off, calling out, "Enjoy that wine, Brenda. We'll catch up more later."

She would enjoy the wine. She'd also enjoy staring both at the picturesque island town of Coupeville, which sprawled before them, and watching the generation of McLaughlins who'd all found their own happily ever afters.

Life was good indeed.

The End

The McLaughlins

Book 1: *One More Round*
Ian McLaughlin's story

Book 2: *Straight, No Chaser*
Colin McLaughlin's story

Book 3: *Top Shelf*
Kenzie McLaughlin's story

Book 4: *Last Call*
Aleck McLaughlin's story

Available now at your favorite online retailer!

About the Author

Shelli is a New York Times and USA Today Bestselling Author who read her first romance novel when she snatched it off her mother's bookshelf at the age of eleven. One taste and she was forever hooked. It wasn't until many years later that she decided to pursue writing stories of her own. By then she acknowledged the voices in her head didn't make her crazy, they made her a writer.

Shelli is a true pluviophile (lover of rain) and currently lives in the Pacific Northwest with her husband and two daughters. She writes various genres of romance, but is most known for her contemporary series such as Holding Out for a Hero, The McLaughlins, and A is for Alpha. She's a compulsive volunteer, and has been known to spontaneously burst into song.

Visit her website at ShelliStevens.com

Thank you for reading

Last Call

If you enjoyed this book, you can find more from all our great authors at TulePublishing.com, or from your favorite online retailer.

Made in the USA
Monee, IL
27 March 2022